THE INVISIBLE PEOPLE

A Novel
by Jeremiah Moon

THE INVISIBLE PEOPLE

Cover design by Jeremiah Moon
First Edition
Published by
BusinessEd4Kids LLC

www.jeremiahmoon.com
For rights, media, or speaking inquiries, contact:

Jeremy@jeremiahmoon.com
Library of Congress Control Number: 2025919171

ISBN: 979-8-9924448-3-4
Printed in the Wellington, FL, USA
August 2025

EPIGRAPH

DEDICATION

To my Beta Readers — Kevin, David, Shane, & Shima — thank you for your support, invaluable feedback, and for being my very first fans.

To the unseen—
those erased by systems,
forgotten by streets,
rewritten by silence.
May your memories endure.
May they anchor the truth.

TABLE OF CONTENTS

FOREWORD

In crafting *The Invisible People*, I drew from shadows close to home—the quiet disappearances of the unhoused, the mental health crises swept beneath corporate rugs, and the digital erasures of an age obsessed with optimization.

Set against a 2025 Florida backdrop, this story asks how easily society "edits" the inconvenient—and what's lost when we accept those edits as normal. But it is also a reminder: memory is resistance.

If you have ever felt unseen, overlooked, or forgotten, know this—your story matters.

This expanded edition deepens Ava's journey, stitching new fragments into the corridors of memory, identity, and choice. Some loops close. Others remain. But every echo is part of the truth we carry forward.

Thank you for reading—
and for remembering.

— *Jeremiah Moon*

THE INVISIBLE PEOPLE

BEFORE THE GLITCH

1

Ava Chen

The first time Ava saw someone disappear, she didn't realize that's what she was seeing. She thought he was just walking away, his silhouette fading into the haze of a West Palm morning, swallowed by the city's relentless churn. But memory works like that sometimes—not with clarity, but with condensation, a misting over of logic. Edges blur, but the pressure lingers, heavy, insistent. The heat of it. The *wrongness*, like a song played in the wrong key, its notes jarring against the silence of what should have been.

It was July 2022, a Florida morning that smelled of heat hours before the sun clawed over West Palm's jagged rooflines, their silhouettes etched against a sky bruised with humidity. The air seeped through her apartment's cracks like an overstaying houseguest, thick, uninvited, carrying the weight of a storm that refused to break. The window unit rattled, coughing its last breath, a mechanical death rattle that echoed the city's faltering pulse. Outside, cicadas droned, their hum weaving into the faint buzz of a streetlight that hadn't shut off since last night's storm, its light flickering like a signal struggling to connect. The air felt charged, electric, as if the world were buffering, caught in a loop it couldn't escape.

Ava stood barefoot in the hallway, the tiles cool against her soles, watching her brother Caleb on the couch. He sat shirtless, legs curled in his awkward half-lotus, a pose he'd claimed since high school "unlocked his brain," though she'd always teased it just made him look like a pretzel with a purpose. His spine slouched, as if gravity pressed harder on him than most, a weight she could almost see bending his shoulders. A battered spiral notebook rested on his knees, its edges frayed from years of being carried, dropped, reclaimed, its pages a testament to his refusal to let go. His pencil danced—frenetic, precise, chasing something only he could see, each stroke a desperate bid to capture a truth the world kept rewriting.

She'd learned not to interrupt these trances. Breaking them cost him something—a spark, a thread, whatever tethered him to himself in a life that seemed determined to unravel him. As a journalist at the *Palm Coast Herald*, chasing bylines on housing scams and city council coverups, she'd once tried to pry into his sketches, thinking they hid a story, a lead that could break open the world's secrets. "You're wasting your talent," she'd told him years ago, half-teasing, half-pleading, her voice catching on the hope he'd hear her. He'd grinned, that lopsided smile that ached for the kid who hid riddles in her library books, who'd once mapped their backyard stars with a flashlight and a dream. Now, his eyes were shadowed, his hands trembling as they worked, and she wondered how much of that boy was left.

"Caleb, you'll burn out that pencil," she said, keeping her voice light, though it trembled at the edges, betraying her fear of losing him to whatever pulled at his mind.

He didn't look up, his focus locked on the page. "A doorway," he murmured. "From a dream. One of the... good ones."

She crossed to the kitchen, tiles cool against her soles, and opened the fridge: half a bottle of cold brew, an orange, two eggs meant for yesterday, their shells dull under the flickering fluorescent light that cast jagged shadows across the counter. She glanced at Caleb, his dark curls matted with lemon balm and sleep, undercut by the faint scent of graphite dust and something metallic—chemical, like the air before a circuit shorts, a warning she couldn't quite name. Her fingers tightened on the fridge handle, the hum of the appliance unsteady, as if it, too, were struggling to hold its place in reality.

Leaning over his shoulder, she studied the drawing: an impossibly tall, narrow archway, its proportions defying physics, a structure that seemed to bend space itself. No door. No hinges. Just lines—layered, interwoven, recursive, twisting like Möbius strips, never lifting, giving an illusion of infinite depth while staying flat. At the base, a symbol she'd fear long after: $\nabla//\psi$, its lines sharp as a blade, pulsing with a meaning she couldn't grasp. Her stomach clenched, a visceral warning. "It's a trap," she said instinctively, her voice low, as if speaking too loudly might summon it.

"It's a way out," Caleb replied, voice soft but certain, his eyes glinting with a fire she hadn't seen in months.

"Looks like both," she countered, folding her arms, her heart quickening as she tried to anchor herself in his presence.

For a beat, only the AC's hum and the pencil's scratch filled the silence, a fragile truce between them and the world outside. Then his smile—soft, tired, fragile—tore at her, reminding her of who he used to be: the boy mapping constellations in their backyard, the man whispering dreams like secrets the stars had told him, before meds dulled his edges, before the halfway house became his address, before he hid food under his bed instead of eating it. She wanted to reach out, to pull him back, but his focus held him like a tether to another reality.

"You used to draw planets," she said, voice catching, a plea disguised as memory. "Now it's... what? Portals?"

He tapped the sketch's edge, his fingers trembling. "If I find this place, I'll send you a postcard," he said, the words light but heavy with something unspoken, a promise she didn't trust him to keep.

She laughed, but it snagged in her throat, sharp and raw. Something about the drawing—*no, the way he drew it*—unnerved her, as if he sketched from memory, not imagination, as if he'd seen that archway in a place she couldn't follow. She poured coffee, its bitterness grounding her, trying to shake the feeling. It clung, sharp and sour, like the aftertaste of a story she couldn't write, a truth she wasn't ready to face. The fridge hummed too loud, then cut out, the silence heavier than it should have been. The air flickered—not the lights, but reality itself, like a bad render in a video game, a glitch that made her skin crawl. She blinked, and it stabilized, but the wrongness lingered, a whisper in her bones.

West Palm was full of anomalies lately—traffic lights blinking out of sync, ATMs spitting blank receipts, her phone dropping calls mid-sentence, as if the city were forgetting how to function, its systems fraying at the edges. She told herself it was nothing, just the chaos of a place stretched too thin by redevelopment, by promises of progress that never quite landed. But deep down, she knew it was more, a pattern she couldn't yet name.

That was a week before Caleb disappeared.

Ava's week dissolved into deadlines and missed deadlines, a blur of words and leads that felt like chasing ghosts. She'd been working a scoop at the *Herald* about NeuroWave, a biotech startup claiming to implant "predictive empathy" in high-stress workplaces—vaporware built on buzzwords and half-patents, a story that should have lit her up, sent her digging through patent filings and whistleblower DMs. Once, such leads had been her lifeblood, each byline a step toward proving herself, toward anchoring her place in a world that seemed to shift beneath her. Now, they felt hollow, like chasing someone else's story, someone else's truth. She spent nights scrolling city webcams, their grainy feeds flickering on her laptop, searching for... what? An anomaly. A signal. A pattern. She wasn't sure, but the need to look gnawed at her, a hunger she couldn't name.

Her inbox overflowed—tips, PR blasts, rants from a guy swearing the mayor was a lizard, his emails a familiar nuisance she deleted without reading. One message stood out, arriving at 2:37 a.m. the night Caleb vanished, when sleep was a distant memory. No sender. No IP trace. Just a subject line: *He's not gone. Just optimized.* The body chilled her, each line a blade cutting through her defenses:

When they reappear,
They won't remember you.
They will seem better.
Cleaner.
But they are not the same.
And neither are you.
— $\nabla//\psi$

No attachments. No threats. Just that symbol, $\nabla//\psi$, pulsing on her screen, though she knew it wasn't animated, its lines sharp as a warning she couldn't ignore. She stared for ten minutes, heart thudding, her apartment's silence pressing down like a weight. She slammed the laptop shut, telling herself it was spam, a cruel prank. West Palm was weird, the internet weirder, a cesspool of creeps and conspiracies. A coincidence, nothing more.

Until Mrs. Delgado called that evening, her voice high, unsteady, not her usual clipped tone. "Ava, it's Caleb's apartment. A neighbor heard banging last night, lights flickering, like someone was tearing the place apart. I checked today. His door was locked from the inside, but... he's not there."

Ava's breath caught, sharp as glass. "What do you mean, not there?"

"I used my key. The place is empty. Bed's a mess, tea's still warm, but no Caleb. Should I call the police?"

Ava grabbed her keys, her hands trembling, the metal biting her palm. "I'm coming over."

She sprinted three blocks, pulse hammering, the humid air clawing at her lungs. Caleb's room was untouched—bed unmade, sheets tangled as if he'd just left, his sketchbook open to that archway, its lines taunting her with their impossible depth. A cup of tea sat on the table, faintly warm, its steam curling like a question mark. No break-in. No struggle. The deadbolt engaged from inside, a puzzle with no solution. One window was cracked an inch, letting in humid air and nothing else. A faint mark on the sill caught her eye— $\nabla//\psi$, scratched into the paint, barely visible unless you knew to look, its lines pulsing with a menace she couldn't shake.

Gone.

The police arrived an hour later, polite, efficient, detached, their voices flat as they scribbled notes. "He's an adult," they said, their eyes sliding past her, as if she, too, were fading. "People leave. Especially with... a history."

"No note?" they asked, their pens hovering, already moving on.

She signed the missing person report, hand shaking, the pen too heavy, carrying the weight of his absence, of a world that seemed to have erased him. That night, she reopened the email, its words no longer spam but a warning, a truth she couldn't unsee. The symbol ▽//ψ burned in her mind, a watermark on reality itself.

Two months later, she saw him.

On Clematis Street, juggling overpriced vegan groceries and a cold brew sweating through its cup, the city's glare harsh against her eyes, she glimpsed him across the street. Same loping walk, the one she'd teased him for, saying he moved like a stray dog with a purpose. Same slouched shoulders, carrying the weight of a world he couldn't map. Same cheekbone scar from a skateboarding crash at sixteen, the one he'd laughed off, saying it gave him character. The mole below his left ear—Caleb always said it made his face *his*, a mark no one could take.

But this man wasn't her Caleb. He wore a tailored blazer, moved with a purpose she didn't recognize, carried a sleek tablet that gleamed in the sun. Smart glasses shimmered, reflecting a skyline too clean, too perfect, a West Palm that didn't exist. He was polished, smoothed, as if someone had run the brother she loved through software, stripping away his edges, his flaws, his *him*. Her gut screamed his name. *Caleb?*

"Caleb?" she whispered, her voice swallowed by the wind and traffic, the city's pulse drowning her out.

She crossed the street, heart racing faster than her steps, groceries
bouncing, coffee spilling down her wrist, staining her sleeve like blood.
"Caleb!" she called louder, her voice cracking, a plea to the air.

He paused mid-step, a beat too long, his head tilting—exactly as
Caleb did, catching a distant sound, like a song only he heard, a habit
she'd loved for its quiet quirk. Her breath caught, hope and dread tan-
gling in her chest.

Then he walked on, faster, turning onto Datura Street, melting into
the pedestrian stream, a shadow slipping through reality's cracks. She
ran, groceries bouncing, coffee splashing, her boots pounding asphalt
that felt too smooth, too new. She rounded the corner.

Gone.

Not lost in the crowd. Not ducked into a store. *Gone*, as if the city
had pressed delete, leaving only a flicker of static where he'd been.
Cleaner. Sharper. A version of Caleb she didn't know, presentable in a
way that made her stomach turn.

That night, Ava didn't sleep. At her kitchen table, eyes red, she
wrote *Caleb* forty times in a blank notebook, pressing the pen hard, as if
ink could anchor him to reality, could keep him from slipping into
whatever void had claimed him. By sunrise, the pages looked like a desperate spell, each letter a plea against forgetting, a shield against the
city's relentless editing. Her hands trembled, the pen slipping, leaving
smudges that felt like failures.

The next morning, she marched into the *Herald* newsroom, a ghost
with a mission, her steps heavy with purpose. She pitched to her editor,

Dan, her voice steady despite the quake in her chest: "My brother disappeared. I saw him again. He didn't recognize me. He wasn't the same."

Dan blinked slowly, intellectual disinterest wafting like cheap cologne, his eyes scanning her like she was a story he didn't want to print. She handed him the email printout, its lines stark against the page.

He skimmed it, shrugged, his voice flat. "Anything traceable? Metadata?"

"No," she said, her throat tight.

"Photos?"

"No."

"Then it's not provable," he said, already turning away.

He let her write it anyway. Twice. Ava buried herself in drafts, chasing threads, drawing timelines, finding eerie overlaps: missing persons reports spiking in West Palm, strange sightings of "returned" people—polished, perfect, unrecognizable, their faces smoothed like avatars in a game no one admitted to playing. She marked patterns, anomalies, that symbol: $\nabla//\psi$—spray-painted on dumpsters, etched into sidewalk gum, glitching in app UIs, a watermark on reality that no one else saw. Her fingers trembled as she typed, the keyboard's clatter a lifeline to something solid.

Her second draft included forum photos—threads on "phantom returns," people who vanished and reappeared "better," cleaner, polite, efficient, *erased*. She printed it on ivory paper, slid it under Dan's door, her heart pounding with the hope it would make him see.

The next morning, he pulled her aside, his voice soft with pity, a tone that cut deeper than dismissal. "You need time off," he said, his eyes avoiding hers.

"It's real," she whispered, her voice breaking, a plea to be believed.

"Maybe," he said. "But it's not readable."

The Invisible People

HR offered tissues and a work-life balance pamphlet, their smiles practiced, detached. She declined therapy, accepted unpaid leave, didn't argue, her silence a shield against their pity. She walked out of the newsroom, the weight of her press badge heavy in her pocket, a relic of a life that no longer fit.

At home, she opened a laptop folder: *Unseen Threads*. She collected everything: screenshots of message boards blinking offline mid-scroll, street-cam stills of pedestrians freezing mid-frame, photos of "returned" missing persons—smoothed avatars of their former selves, their eyes empty of the people they'd been. The symbol— $\nabla//\psi$ — emerged like a fingerprint on reality's lens: in a ride-share app's code, on a receipt, faintly burned into a dollar bill, its lines pulsing with a menace she couldn't ignore. *It wasn't just* **his** *mark. It was* **theirs**.

She told herself it was grief, weaving patterns from shadows, gods from coincidences, a mind desperate to make sense of loss. But one night, her hallway light flickered—once, again, then stabilized, the silence heavier than it should have been. In the stillness, she felt it: the postcard. Not paper. Not ink. Not real. But *sent*, a message from a place she couldn't name, a tether to Caleb that refused to break.

Her chest tightened, her breath shallow. She whispered into the dark: "If you're still out there…" She didn't finish, didn't need to. The words hung, a prayer unanswered but alive.

In the years since, Ava traded her press badge for a coffee apron on Clematis Street, its weight lighter, safer, quieter, less likely to mark her as unstable in a world that preferred her silent. She poured cold brew, frothed oat milk for tourists who thought West Palm was up-and-coming, crafted latte art like it mattered, each swirl a small act of defiance against a reality that kept shifting. But the anomalies never stopped. A crosswalk sign switching to *DON'T WALK* mid-step, its red glow too sharp, too deliberate. Graffiti in her handwriting she'd never written, scrawled on walls that hadn't been there yesterday. A child with eyes too old, staring too long, as if they saw the cracks she couldn't name.

And always, that symbol—$\nabla//\psi$—reappearing like a fingerprint on her life's lens, sometimes in plain sight, sometimes only on a second glance, its lines a silent warning of a world being rewritten. She called it coincidence, paranoia, trauma, but deep down, Ava knew: *The editing had only begun.*

STATIC RESIDUE

2

Ava Chen

The streetlight outside her building buzzed again.
Not a flicker—
a buzz.
Low. Jagged.
Like frayed wires trying to speak in a language she almost recognized.

Ava stopped beneath it, coffee cup trembling in her hand. The heat bled out quick, just like her shift, leaving her with nothing but the stain of espresso on her apron and the ache in her shoulders.

The city was wrong tonight.
Too still.
No cars idling. No palms whispering in the wind. Even her phone stayed dark in her pocket—no pings, no spam, not even phantom alerts.

Jeremiah Moon

The quiet pressed in like someone's hand on her mouth.
It wasn't natural.
It was deliberate.

Her lips moved before her mind caught up.

"Reflection containment. Phase one."

She froze. The words weren't hers. Or—maybe they were, but from a part of her she didn't remember.

The buzz answered back a half-beat late, as though her voice had been copied, delayed, and played through the lamp.

Ava forced her feet forward. She didn't want to go home yet—not to Caleb's empty chair, not to the silence that remembered him better than she could. She walked for motion's sake, telling herself she could outrun grief. She knew better. Grief had longer legs.

The burned-out diner drew her. Its charred ribs had loomed for months, half a ruin, half a warning. Tonight, a green pulse glowed from inside. Not firelight. Not life. Emergency exit signs, stubborn in a place no one had entered for years.

The air thickened—ash and ozone, storm-scent without rain. The half-melted OPEN sign twitched, but wrong, each flicker a syncopation against her pulse.

Her boots scuffed pavement that felt too smooth, too new. Polished over.
Like someone had replaced the ground while she wasn't looking.
And then—him.

Cross-legged in the alley beyond the dumpster, notebook propped on his knees, pencil cutting frantic lines like each mark kept the world from slipping apart.

Her throat tightened. The outline was familiar. Too familiar. "Maps?" she whispered.

The figure lifted his head. Eddie Morales's face—but drained, younger, eyes hollowed and glinting like cracked glass catching moonlight. When his lips moved, the voice that came out wasn't his.

It was hers.

Her own voice.

Thrown back, sharpened.

"Anchors don't hold unless remembered."

Ava's stomach dropped. Her chest clenched as if the air had turned into static. "Who are you?"

A faint smile cut across his face, all sorrow and apology. He turned the notebook toward her.

Her own bathroom mirror stared back.

Split down the middle.

One half of her face screaming.

The other half smiling.

"You haven't broken yet," he said, voice soft, almost kind. "But she has."

The pronoun hit like a stone to the gut. Caleb's sketches rushed back—doors that weren't doors, archways that bent the rules of space, the promise he'd never keep: *If I find it, I'll send you a postcard.*

The alley lurched sideways, shadow and light sliding like wet paint on glass. His body stuttered, pixelated, phasing in and out. He tried to speak again—

"...re...mem...ber..."

The notebook snapped shut. His outline shredded into static.

Gone.

Only the buzz remained, lower now, meaner, vibrating along her spine like residue in her nerves.

Ava stumbled backward, then ran. Her boots struck asphalt too perfect to be trusted. By the time she burst into her apartment, her lungs burned, but the room inside was eerily normal. Too normal.

The couch sagged where Caleb had always sat.

The fridge hummed steady.

The air smelled scrubbed, chemical-clean, like someone had erased her from it.

Then she saw it.

Her toothbrush.

Wet.

Bristles splayed.

She hadn't touched it tonight.

Her skin went cold.

The mirror over the sink fogged, though no shower steamed. She stepped closer, heart slamming against her ribs.

The reflection leaned forward first.

Anticipating.

Rehearsing her.

Her lips parted. The voice that came out was hers—but not.

Sharper.

"Red corridor opened early. Don't go alone."

Ava staggered back, shoulder cracking against the doorframe, pain enough to hold her for one breath.

The notebook on the table—Caleb's old one, the one that shouldn't move—flipped itself open. Pages fluttered in a panic, then stopped.

On the blank paper, words etched themselves in graphite lines too jagged to be hers:

DRIFT SIGNATURE LOGGED. TAG: 001-A – PRE-BLEED ALERT.

Her throat caught. She wanted to scream but clamped a hand over her mouth.

"This isn't real," she whispered into her palm. But the room bent at the edges, reality wobbling like a reel skipping frames.

She blinked.

She was upright in bed. Sheets twisted around her legs. Moonlight striping the floor.

A dream. Probably.

Her gaze slid to the nightstand. The notebook waited there. Closed. Safe.

Except—one page corner had been folded outward. A marker.

Her breath hitched. She lifted her hands. Graphite dust streaked her fingertips.

Not a dream.

The city's silence vibrated faintly, as though waiting for her to take the next step.

INTERLUDE: OPERATOR LOG – PRECURSOR INTERCEPT

Equinox Initiative // Mirror Watch Subnet – Field Terminal Record

Operator ID: ███████-2739
Clearance Tier: Observation-Only // Drift Passive
Timestamp: T–037:19:02 Prior to Glitch Alpha

[LOG OPENED]

Subject of Note: Chen, Ava
Thread Classification: Observer-Class Candidate (Unverified)
Behavioral Flag: Micro-loop resistance / pre-drift awareness spikes
Environmental Stability Index: 97.2% – Within acceptable echo-tension margins
Interruption Source: Unknown. Artifact origin possible.

Field Notes:

At 02:18 local, subject engaged in unprompted surveillance contact.
CCTV node: Clematis Street, Zone B-17.
Her gaze fixed on lens pulse. Duration: 3.4 seconds. Intentional. Sustained.
Pupil dilation inconsistent with ambient lux readings. Suggestive of spectrum recognition outside visual range.

Audio capture – subvocalization event:

[Clip Tag: 42_chen_subvocal.AIFF]
Transcript (filtered): *"I don't like this version."*
Recipient unknown. Self-directed? Or addressed outward? Signal cadence aligned with call-and-response patterns. Not random.
Immediately following: silhouette distortion. Glass-bend shimmer, not heat haze. Logged as **Possible Echo Overlap – Pre-Merge Drift (Unscheduled).**

Diagnostics:
- No breach signatures.
- No active memory leaks.
- No catalogued prior exposures.

Yet: subject's path through Zone B-17 left latent shimmer trace. Corridor physics bending in her presence. Subjects are not meant to notice until directed. She noticed *before*.

Recommendation: Silent tag only. *No engagement. No adjust-ment.*
Risk curve: Intervention amplifies resistance exponentially.

Operator Commentary [Tier 3 Encrypted]:
I do not trust this one.
Not for hostility.
For awareness.
She writes in margins. Hears hum beneath silence. Dreams in directions that do not align.
Her footprints in B-17 read like wet concrete: permanent, wrong, visible even when scrubbed.
She is not simply a candidate. She is a fracture.
Fractures do not scale. They split. They spread.
She will collapse early—swallowed by drift pressure. Or she will force rewrite.
And the system does not tolerate rewrites.

[LOG TERMINATED]
Checksum: $\nabla//\psi$

THE ONE YOU FORGOT

PROLOGUE

Maps

The city remembered everything except him.

It cataloged bus schedules and potholes, balanced budget shortfalls into neat columns, and tracked power surges down to the second. But Maps Morales? It let him slip. He sat on the same corner, day after day, a man trying to hold a West Palm that refused to stay still, its streets shifting like a dream bleeding at the edges.

He knew the sidewalk under him wasn't steady. Concrete trembled like it was buffering. Some mornings he wondered if *he* was buffering, too.

His pencil scraped across the battered notebook in his lap. The spine was patched with duct tape, the pages swollen by years of damp air. They weren't just maps anymore. They were layers—sketches over diagrams, graffiti turned to coordinates, margins filled with hands he didn't remember writing with. Some lines shimmered faintly in dawn's light, pulsing like veins beneath paper. They shouldn't have been real. But they were—more real than the city that kept trying to forget him.

Today, the streets buzzed wrong again. Not in his head. In his teeth. An old filling vibrated with static, a second heartbeat knocking under his skull. The skyline leaned, just enough to tilt his stomach, a conspiracy drawn in glass and concrete.

He had once been Eddie Morales. An urban planner. Crisp suits, clean diagrams, GIS lectures at the library that made kids doze but gave him pride. He had believed in numbers, in shaping a city with logic. Until one morning a blueprint on his desk had changed. Overnight. A park erased. A ramp drawn in its place.

He showed his supervisor. She smiled, puzzled.
"What park?"

That was the first time he learned: if the city forgot, everyone else did too. And the ones who remembered? They didn't stay.

Now he mapped by hand, graphite-stained fingers tracing fractures only he could see.

Bootsteps echoed—a cadence he knew. Ava. She left food sometimes, coffee others. A tether he didn't know how to thank. Tonight she crouched beside him. Her shadow flickered wrong, edges splitting, doubling, then stitching back together as though the air hadn't decided which version of her to keep.

"They moved the crosswalk again," she murmured.

Maps didn't look up. His pencil trembled. "No," he whispered. "They moved a version of us."

Her breath caught. "Version of what?"

21

"Of here," he said. "Of you."

His hand jerked—unbidden. Lines carved themselves onto the page: $\nabla//\psi$. Sharp. Familiar. The same mark that haunted overlays, Equinox crashes, every erased photo. His chest tightened. And with it came the smell—ozone, burning solder, as if someone had fried the air.

A bus hissed at the corner. Its doors snapped shut, too loud, too final. When it pulled away, Ava looked down.

Maps was gone. Notebook gone.

Only a crack remained in the sidewalk, fresh, pulsing once like a heartbeat before falling still.

The static—no, the residue—pressed against her skin. Heavy. Alive.

Ava stood frozen, coffee cooling in her hand, feeling the city edit itself around her. Caleb had been the first loss.

Maps wouldn't be the last.

CRACKS IN THE SIDEWALK

3

Ava Chen

The sidewalk cracked again—a seam splitting the concrete like a wound the city refused to heal. Ava stumbled, coffee sloshing over her knuckles, her boots catching on the raised edge. A man in a wrinkled suit jacket passed, earbuds dangling like loose wires, casting her a glance that registered nothing. In West Palm, no one cared unless blood stained the pavement. And even then, only if the shoes were worth noticing.

She crouched, lacing her boot. Her fingertips traced the break. Too clean. No weeds pushing through. No gum fossilized in the groove. A scar without history. The warmth of the two cups steadied her hands, but not the unease tightening in her chest.

It wasn't the crack itself that rattled her. It was the betrayal of memory—her body remembering this block differently, like the street had shifted while she slept. It was happening more often: crosswalks sliding, traffic lights out of rhythm, doors opening on the wrong side of buildings. She'd blamed grief. Fatigue. Caleb gone. Maps fading. But today it felt deliberate. Too sharp to be chance.

Above her, a billboard hummed. A man in a navy suit smiled against a skyline scrubbed of dirt, cracks, scars.

Reimagine Your Potential.

His grin was smooth. Synthetic. The kind of face you got when flaws were erased. Ava turned away, boots scuffing on asphalt that felt too new underfoot.

The alley revealed itself only when she was nearly past it. Static thickened the air, ozone tangled with the stench of burned wiring.

Eddie "Maps" Morales sat hunched on a crate, notebook open on his knees. Graphite stained his fingers. His shadow bent wrong against the wall, stretching at angles the sun couldn't account for.

"Haven't seen you in a few days," Ava said carefully.

Maps's voice came out gravel-rough, but steady. "Didn't feel like being where they expected me."

She offered him a cup. "Extra cream."

He sniffed it, sipped. "Cinnamon again. You never change."

Her lips twitched. "You're still breathing. You're still drinking coffee."

For a second, something softened in him. A ghost of a smile. "Guess that makes two of us."

Relief eased her chest.

"They shifted the crosswalk again," he muttered, pencil stabbing the page. A red circle glared back, gridlines skewed. Beside it: $\nabla//\psi$.

Ava frowned. "How do you know?"

"My bones know the old way," he said. "My eyes tell the lie."

Her pulse skipped. "Ever say a word and it suddenly feels… wrong?"

Maps gave a dry laugh, no humor in it. "Déjà vu in reverse. They aren't making anything new. Just overwriting what we already had."

She hesitated. "Who's they?"

"Curators. Architects. Equinox—whatever name they're wearing this week." He snapped his pencil and didn't flinch, pulling another from his coat pocket. "Doesn't matter. They edit. Always safer to erase than build."

The words cut her deeper than she expected.

She crouched closer, coffee warming her palms. "That sounds insane."

His eyes lifted to hers, and in them wasn't dismissal, but something harder: conviction. "So does memory—until it's gone."

The notebook showed a doorway sketched in impossible geometry.

Equinox Node – Trap Entry.

"Why draw this?" she whispered.

"Paper doesn't lie to itself," he said. His tone roughened, but when he glanced at her again, it softened. "You're seeing it too, aren't you?"

Her throat tightened. "I think so."

"Then don't just see. Anchor it," he said, gentler this time, gravel turning to warning. "Before it slips."

The steam from his cup lingered too long, coiling in the air like a glitch pretending to be breath.

"You ever think you're the glitch?" she asked.

25

Maps's laugh cracked, brittle. "I used to. But the system's too clean for accidents like me." He looked at her longer, voice quiet now. "But you—people like you don't just glitch. You... shift. And shifts matter."

Her chest ached at the way he said it, like he already knew how much she'd lose.

At the curb, the alley's shadow stretched farther than the sun allowed. She blinked. It didn't retreat.

Back on the street, the billboard glitched again. Same smile. New words:

You didn't see them before.
You won't recognize them now.

Her pulse jumped. A blink later, the ad reset.

No one else noticed.

She hugged her coffee close, walking faster, sidewalk trembling beneath her like memory itself was cracking.

Her phone buzzed. An app she didn't recall installing pulsed across the screen:

Update Available: Memory Optimization.

She swiped it away, thumb trembling. But the icon stayed.

$\nabla//\psi$.

Faint. Waiting.

RESIDUAL PULSE

4

Caleb Chen (Echo Variant)

Caleb hadn't dreamed in weeks. Or maybe he had, but the dreams weren't his. They arrived already fragmented — jagged sketches filling his notebook before he was awake enough to claim them, words scrawled in graphite strokes that curved like warnings. Some mornings, he found himself gripping a pencil he didn't remember lifting. Other mornings, he woke standing in the middle of the room, heart pounding, sweat cooling on his chest as if he'd been running from something that wasn't there.

The shakes always came first. They had once belonged to withdrawal — familiar, ugly companions that Ava had pulled him through, holding his hands still when nothing else could. Now they were back, but different. Not the gnawing ache of absence, not the hollow craving for chemicals, but a tremor in the air itself, crawling through his bones like static. It wasn't just him anymore. It was the world.

He sat at the edge of his bed, staring at the floor until the planks blurred into a single trembling line. His notebook lay open on the table across the room, its battered spine cracked wide. A fresh drawing filled the page: a corridor with no end, its walls bending inward, lined with doors that carried no handles. He reached for memory, trying to catch the moment he had sketched it. Nothing. Only the echo of graphite rasping across paper and a whisper in his head that hadn't been his own.

Caleb dragged his hands across his face, fingers cold against his eyes. He wanted to believe exhaustion was enough to explain it. Too little sleep. Too much coffee. His sister's absence digging a hollow behind his ribs that no substance could fill. But the truth pulsed deeper. He felt it in the silence between seconds.

The mirror above the sink caught him when he stood, pulling him closer with the weight of recognition. His reflection met him with its usual posture — shoulders slouched, hair unkempt, the small scar at his eyebrow from a half-forgotten skateboarding fall. Familiar. Almost. But the eyes weren't his. They were older. Heavier. Staring at him with the sorrow of someone who had already lost more than he could imagine.

Caleb leaned closer. The reflection hesitated before moving, just a fraction of a second, but enough to curdle his stomach. He raised his hand, palm out, bracing for the cold press of glass. Instead, warmth bled back into his skin. A faint pulse throbbed beneath the surface, steady, alive. The mirror had a heartbeat.

He snatched his hand back, heart hammering. His breaths came in shallow bursts. "No. No, no, no…" The word felt like a mantra, but it had no power.

He turned away, rubbing his trembling fingers down his jeans. Ava would have held them still. She used to sit with him when the shakes came, thumb brushing across his knuckles, grounding him with stubborn love that refused to bend. Without her, the tremor belonged only to him.

On the table sat something worse than the mirror: a photograph.

It shouldn't have existed. Ava, caught mid-laugh. Her head tilted back, eyes bright, joy unguarded in a way he hadn't seen in years. The edges were creased as if folded and unfolded a hundred times. He picked it up, feeling the texture of the paper — too real, too deliberate.

When had this been taken? Her hair was shorter. The lighting wrong, harsh in ways their apartment never was. He stared, trying to pin it down. The longer he looked, the more the picture flickered. An earring appeared. Vanished. The line of her jaw sharpened, then softened again.

But the laughter stayed. He could hear it, not through memory, but alive, pulsing in his head like the photograph had stolen sound from the past.

Caleb pressed a thumb to the crease. The paper quivered. His stomach lurched. "Is this mine?" he whispered. His voice cracked. "Or hers?"

The room hummed in answer. Not the fridge. Not the lights. The air. A low vibration crawled along his ribs, slipping into his bones until every breath stuttered with it.

Static disguised as silence.

It reminded him of detox nights — body gnawing at itself, ears filled with phantom sounds that never stopped. Only this wasn't withdrawal. This was the world unraveling around him.

His phone buzzed against the counter. No number. No name. Just a text:

Red corridor blinked.
Subject: Ava Chen.
Anchor logged.
Residual thread syncing.

He froze, staring at the words. They were nonsense. Yet each one landed heavy in his chest. Ava. Always Ava. His anchor and his undoing, the tether that had dragged him through hell and still held fast in a city determined to forget.

He clenched the phone until the edges bit into his palm. The pain was proof. Proof that this moment belonged to him, not some flicker of memory they'd stolen.

The hallway outside his door stretched wrong.

He stepped into it cautiously. The light was too bright. The air too still. He counted doors. One, two, three—fifteen. His apartment building had six. He counted again, desperate for a mistake, for fatigue to explain what he saw. The number didn't change.

The wallpaper peeled when he brushed his fingertips along it. Not plaster beneath — ink. Letters unfurling into words. Ava's handwriting twisted into coordinates he couldn't read. They writhed under his touch, alive, accusing. His chest tightened. The taste of metal filled his mouth, sharp as blood.

He blinked.

The hallway shifted.

Threadbare carpet underfoot, the sour reek of mildew filling his nostrils. Fluorescent lights buzzed like dying insects.

He blinked again.

Sterile white walls. Steel doors marked B-7, B-8, B-9. His sleeve flickered — plaid, black, plaid again.

And always the photograph in his pocket. Ava laughing. Ava stern. Blank paper. Each version slicing him differently, refusing to settle.

Caleb pressed the photo flat against his chest, as if holding it there would stop the world from shifting. His breath rattled in his throat.

The last door pulsed with faint light.

He knocked.

The echo sank into him, reverberating too deep, too long, as though the hall itself were hollow bone. The sound didn't fade. It burrowed.

The door opened.

The corridor beyond wasn't one place. It was all of them.

Office fluorescents stretching into infinity. Subway tunnels dripping with condensation. A hospital ward with beds dented from bodies that no longer existed. His childhood bedroom painted in the colors of a life he half-remembered.

Each flickered into the next without transition, as if the world couldn't decide which memory to anchor.

Caleb clutched the photograph tighter. Blank now. Just paper. His chest ached as if the picture had stolen his sister from him again.

He staggered forward, each step landing on a different version of the corridor. Tile became concrete. Carpet became linoleum. The air shifted from hospital disinfectant to subway rust to childhood dust.

The silence thickened. Then Ava's voice broke through.

Faint. Certain.

"Memory isn't just what you keep. It's what keeps you."

His throat closed.

She had said that once. Or maybe she hadn't. Maybe it was the Ava from the photo, or the Ava who laughed in a timeline he no longer owned. He wanted to believe it was her. He wanted to believe she was still reaching for him, still steadying his shaking hands.

Tears burned at the corners of his eyes. He stepped deeper into the corridor anyway, into its pulse.

The world shifted again.

The photo slipped from his fingers, falling without sound.

And the pulse stayed with him.

NOT JUST GONE

5

Ava Chen

The alley was empty.

No blanket. No cart. No Maps.

Ava stood there with a paper cup clutched so tight the lid bent in, steam bleeding upward like a soul slipping free. The spot where Eddie "Maps" Morales had always been—his hunched frame, his frantic pencil—was bare. Not abandoned. Erased.

No footprints pressed into grit. No chewed pencil stub. No notebook with its swollen pages. Nothing.

Her chest constricted.

People don't just vanish twice.

First Caleb. Now Maps.

The Invisible People

The steam stung her eyes as she turned away, forcing her body forward though her stomach screamed to stay, to dig until she found something the city hadn't polished away.

The café was only a block off, but the walk stretched long, like the streets had been copied and pasted wrong.

She keyed the code into the back door, her fingers trembling more than the weather allowed.

Inside, everything hummed too normal. The espresso machine chugged steady. Overhead bulbs flickered with their usual buzz. The playlist—management's "slow jazz, upbeat enough to sell muffins"—played its false cheer. All of it grated, as if the world were insisting on its own sanity just to spite her.

Donnie was at the grinder, his apron streaked, hair gelled too neat for the hour. He looked up. "You look like you saw a ghost, Ava."

"Yeah," she said automatically, voice flat. "Didn't sleep."

He shrugged and tamped grounds into the portafilter. "Want a shot?"

"No." She set her cup on the counter, untouched.

His gaze lingered a beat longer than usual, then he added, "That guy hasn't been around."

Her chest lurched. "What guy?"

"You know. The one out back. Layered clothes. Notebook. Battery-acid smell." He wrinkled his nose. "Camped in that alley like it was rent-controlled."

"Maps," she said, sharper than intended. "Eddie Morales."

Donnie squinted, like the name bounced off him. "If you say so."

"You saw him. You gave him food. A sandwich." She leaned forward, pushing. "Last month, you laughed—said he had 'mad scientist vibes.'"

Donnie shook his head, blank. "Pretty sure I'd remember that."

The casual dismissal landed harder than if he'd yelled.

She pressed on. "You've seen him this week, right?"

He hesitated. Then shrugged. "Nah. People like that… they move on. Right?"

Ava froze. The phrase was too clean, like a script. *People leave.*

For half a second, something in her almost nodded. She pictured Maps walking away, cart squeaking behind him, finding a quieter corner of the city. People do that. They drift.

Her stomach twisted.

No. Not him. He doesn't leave.

The thought slammed back in like a pulse, fierce, defiant.

"No," she said aloud, too sharp. "That alley was his."

Donnie's eyes flickered with something like unease—but then it was gone, smoothed over into his barista autopilot. "Okay," he said, turning back to the machine.

The same tone the cops had used about Caleb.

People leave. Especially with… a history.

On her break, Ava slipped back outside. The alley remained blank.

Her hand shook as she opened her phone gallery. Proof. She *had* proof.

Two weeks ago: Maps crouched on his crate, notebook open, steam rising from the coffee she'd brought him.

She tapped it. The image blinked.

Now it showed nothing. Just the alley. Concrete and a single trash bin. No Maps.

Her chest seized.

She opened another: three months ago. Maps mid-laugh, pencil gripped between his teeth. She zoomed in, desperate for the curve of his mouth, the shine in his eyes.

The pixels warped. Laughter dissolved into static. All that remained was a cup on the ground.

Her throat closed. Her eyes burned. She staggered against the wall, phone trembling in her hand.

She looked up, desperate for someone—anyone—to see what she saw.

But the world went on. Pigeons fought over a crust. A cyclist cursed. A siren flared and faded.

Normal. Except her.

That night, after close, she lingered. The café emptied. Casey, the new girl, left early for class. Donnie locked up and muttered a distracted "See ya."

Alone, Ava slipped behind the counter and pulled up the old security terminal. The cameras weren't good—grainy black-and-white, their timestamps lagging minutes behind real time—but they remembered. Machines remembered.

She scrolled back two nights. Maps should've been there, hunched in his alley kingdom.

Nothing. Just empty concrete.

Her jaw clenched. She knew where to look, the exact angle. She scrubbed backward further. Two weeks. Three.

Each frame showed the same blank space. As if he'd never existed.

Her pulse hammered. She wanted to smash the monitor, force it to bleed the truth. Instead she scrolled forward again, to last week.

And there—her own figure entered the alley. Her hair in a bun, coat collar up. Carrying two cups.

She watched herself crouch. Hand one forward. Talk. Laugh. Nod.

But the space in front of her was empty. She was handing coffee to no one.

Her breath hitched, shallow and ragged.

The footage looped, repeating her gestures into air.

Her mouth shaped words she couldn't hear.

Had she imagined him?

Her fingers dug into her palms until her nails left crescents.

"No," she whispered. "No, he was there. He was there."

Her voice sounded small in the empty café.

When she finally left, the street outside her building felt altered.

The streetlight hummed too steady. The scuff on the third stair was gone. The mail slot glided smoother than it ever had. Small edits, invisible except to someone already fraying.

Am I forgetting it wrong? Or remembering it right?

Inside, she didn't turn on the lights.

The notebook was waiting on the counter.

Maps's. Same battered cover. Same faint coffee stain.

Her heart stopped. She hadn't carried it here. She hadn't touched it.

It lay open. The sketches inside were precise, deliberate. Today's date written in neat script.

Her apartment mapped in clean black lines. Furniture in exact pro-por-tion. Even the crooked leg of her table, rendered perfect.

Her hand went numb.

She glanced at the shelf. Another notebook sat there, dusty, un-moved.

She looked back. The counter copy was gone.

Ava pressed her palms against the sink, fighting for breath. The mirror above caught her reflection—and blinked first.

Her body locked.

She splashed water on her face, the sound echoing too sharp, too clean.

Behind her, a whisper brushed the air. One syllable. Gone before she could catch it.

She turned.

The notebook was open again.

Red ink slashed across the blueprint:

YOU REMEMBERED.

Her lungs seized. Her chest trembled.

This wasn't grief. This wasn't paranoia.

It was a system. Precise. Cold.

Reality being rewritten, one absence at a time.

And if Maps could vanish this cleanly—what chance did she have left?

INTERLUDE: LOOP CALIBRATION

Operator // Tier 3 // Unnamed

[Begin Internal Log // Reflection Thread: AVA-88A // Clearance Tier: Shadow-Level Beta]
Timestamp: ΔT+0004:18 from Initial Corridor Divergence
Observation: Window Opened. Subject unstable. Loop distortion detected.

She shouldn't have resisted the amnesia trigger. Not this early.

Subject Ava Chen, Variant 88A. Retention confirmed after Phase One exposure. Dream-bloom event triggered prematurely. Reflection drift spiked above 0.3%.

Consensus was to let it burn out.
They were wrong.

She retained.
She always retains.
She shouldn't have.

I've tracked her since Thread 42 collapsed—back when she wrote herself out of a merge. Even then she was recursive. Feedback-positive. Loop-defiant.

Loop Sync: Incomplete
Reinforcement: External bleedthrough suspected

There's another node active in her range. Unknown identity.

My guess? Caleb. Not this thread's Caleb—one of the ghosts. A variant that didn't collapse clean.

It's always the ones with emotional drift. They anchor unintentionally. Sync out of grief, or guilt, or unfinished memory. Ava is that type. Dangerous in the way soft things survive.

Numbers confirm it: her Reflection Delay Rate dropped below 0.5s. That means she sees them now. Not directly. Not yet. But enough.

Enough to question the sidewalk cracks again. Enough to follow her own echoes.

Containment Recommendation: Delay further edits. Introduce noise variables. Disrupt sleep cycle.

It won't last. None of it ever does. But the longer we wait, the more entangled she becomes. And if she reconnects with the wrong version—Malik, Caleb, or herself—

Well.

Mirrors crack in more than one direction.

[End Log // Operator Signature Redacted // Observation Ongoing]

STATIC IN THE SYSTEM

6

Ava

Ava didn't sleep that night, her body rigid on the sagging mattress, eyes tracing cracks in the ceiling that seemed to shift in the dark, like veins pulsing beneath West Palm's skin. The fridge's hum was a low growl, unsteady, weaving with the wall clock's uneven tick—slower, then faster, then stuttering, a heartbeat with arrhythmia, as if time itself were glitching. At some point, the power blinked, a fleeting betrayal. Lamps dimmed, the fridge coughed, appliances reset in a chorus of soft clicks. The digital clock by her bed flickered through a blur of numbers, freezing at 3:17, its red glow too sharp, like a warning carved in light. Her phone screen lit without her touch, the Wi-Fi icon dancing—dropped, reappeared, dropped again. Static in the system, a phrase that slipped from her lips, unbidden, heavy with a truth she couldn't name. *Static in the system.* She spoke it aloud, testing its weight, the words feeling borrowed, as if they'd spilled from another mouth, another life she didn't recall living.

By morning, her appetite was gone, replaced by a tension vibrating through her muscles, an echo trying to claw its way into shape. She needed to know—not just what happened to Maps, to Caleb, to the notebook, but to *her*, to the city, to the reality that once felt solid but now buckled like wet cardboard beneath her feet. Her thoughts buzzed, too fast to catch, like a swarm of insects trapped in her skull. She felt like she was walking through someone else's memory of her life, each step a betrayal of the world she thought she knew.

She arrived at the café before opening, the sun clawing over the skyline, its light reluctant, as if unsure it wanted to reveal the city's secrets. The neon sign flickered, its buzz a faint echo of the streetlight's menace from the night before. Donnie was already there, stacking cups into precarious towers, a pyramid of porcelain that seemed to defy gravity, his hands moving with the careless rhythm of someone untouched by the city's shifting edges.

"You're early," he said, glancing up, his eyes narrowing. "You okay?"

"Need to check the alley cam," Ava replied, her voice tight. "Security footage."

Donnie frowned, wiping his hands on his apron. "We get robbed or something?"

"Just weird stuff," she said, forcing calm. "Probably nothing."

He shrugged, handed her the access tablet, its screen smudged with coffee grounds. "Be my guest. Want the music off?"

"No. Leave it."

The Invisible People

The lo-fi jazz filled the room, tinny from ceiling speakers, its notes grating against her nerves like static woven into melody. She slipped into the back office, shutting the door, the air thick with cardboard and cinnamon syrup, a cloying sweetness that didn't belong. A single fluorescent buzzed overhead, flickering like it couldn't decide whether to stay lit, drilling into her temples with each pulse. The tablet booted slowly, as if it doubted what she'd find, the login screen pulsing once, freezing, then letting her in without a password—a glitch that made her stomach lurch.

She scrubbed yesterday's footage: 6:00 a.m., 7:00 a.m., 8:15—there. Her own image walked past the alley, coffee in hand, frozen on the screen while her real self sat rigid, breath shallow. She fast-forwarded: 9:00, 9:05, 9:10. The alley stayed empty. Then—wrong. The timestamp jumped: 9:10:38 → 9:12:41. Two minutes erased, a gap in reality's fabric. Her pulse hammered, a frantic rhythm against her ribs. She rewound, played it again. At 9:10:37, the screen flickered—one frame of static, sharp as a scream.

And there it was. A shape. Maps. Layered in cloth, hunched, half-visible, his scarf's frayed edge unmistakable. Gone in a blink. *They missed a frame.* Her breath hitched, eyes burning as she leaned forward, forehead nearly touching the tablet, the image searing into her like a brand. Her journalist instincts kicked in, muscle memory from a life she'd tried to bury. Five years ago, she'd have had a draft by lunch: *City Cleansing Scandal. Timeline Tampering? Algorithmic Erasure?* She'd covered housing scams, whistleblower vanishings, city councilors laundering votes through zoning loopholes, her bylines sharp enough to cut through lies. But those stories hadn't mattered. Her last front-page exposé was buried under a corporate buyout, the same month Caleb overdosed in a halfway house the city pretended didn't exist. *Overdosed.* The word

44

shifted as she thought it, edges smudging, dates refusing to settle, like a memory repeated until it lost meaning. She pushed it down, as always, but it clawed back, sharper now.

The notebook and coffee apron had replaced her press badge—safer, quieter, less likely to break her again. But this wasn't a story. It was a warning, pulsing like the $\nabla//\psi$ symbol that haunted her dreams. Her hands shook as she exported the corrupted footage to a USB drive, dropping it into her bag like it was radioactive, its weight a tether to a truth no one else would see.

Back at the counter, Donnie slid a coffee across without asking, his eyes lingering too long, as if she'd stepped through a door he didn't want to acknowledge. "You good?" he asked, voice cautious.

"Just a weird glitch," she said, forcing a casual tone. "Probably need to patch the software."

He nodded, but his gaze held a flicker of doubt, like he saw the cracks she couldn't name. During a lull in the rush, Ava pulled up a public-access transit feed on her phone, the video grainy, shadows flickering too much for the time of day. She scrubbed to 9:11 a.m. A bus pulled in. A man stepped off, wearing Maps's scarf—frayed edge, two tassels missing, a faded patch like a coffee stain. Her stomach tightened. She paused, zoomed. The details were unmistakable, identical. She replayed it, slowing the frame. He paused, turned toward the alley, then walked out of frame, as if the city had swallowed him again.

Her throat closed, eyes watering. He was there—after he was gone. She printed the still, clipped it into the notebook, its pages heavy with Caleb's absence. When she flipped it open, the pages had shifted, graphite marking a new page, dark and fresh: a transit map, the station circled in thick strokes, underlined with $\nabla//\psi$. Beneath, a phrase etched so hard the paper dented: *Phase One complete. Drift protocol active.* The paper felt warm, the graphite shimmering in the café's light, a pulse she couldn't ignore.

That night, she ran a reverse image search of the scarf. Nothing. She uploaded the corrupted frame to an AI restorer. The site froze, reloaded, the image gone. She tried again—different device, different network. Same result. Her laptop buzzed once, then powered off, plunging the apartment into silence, the dark pressing in like a living thing. She sat rigid, the notebook's weight anchoring her.

She reached for it, hands trembling. On the inside cover, in handwriting disturbingly like her own: *You were never supposed to see this far.* Her chest seized. She slammed the cover shut, heart hammering. Her phone lit on the table, blank at first, then scrolling: *RECOGNITION CONFIRMED. ANCHOR: CHEN, AVA (NULL-CLASS). STATUS: OBSERVING.* She dropped it, the plastic burning her palm.

She spread the USB, the still, and the notebook across her kitchen table, a constellation of proof no one else would remember. Once, she wrote truth for the city. Now she was fighting to remember it. She flipped to the notebook's back, seeking a blank page. Instead, a list: names, most scratched out. One remained, circled: *Dominic Parr.*

The name sparked nothing, then everything—a flicker, pigeons scattering in a burst of feathers, a man's hand breaking bread on a street corner. She shook her head, the images slipping like static. Another flash: a muttered voice, low, steady, words drifting as if to no one—or to birds on a railing. Her chest tightened, the fragments too real to dismiss. Next to the name, in hard strokes: *Returned.*

Ava copied *Dominic Parr* onto a sticky note, her hand shaking. Tomorrow, she'd find him. Maps was gone. Caleb was gone. But she was still here. And she remembered. In a world forgetting itself, that felt like the most dangerous act of all.

PARR'S GHOST

7

Dominic Parr

The pigeons never lied.

That was why Dominic fed them. Every morning, every evening, scraps stolen or begged, stale bread torn into neat little pieces. He liked the way they swarmed, the rhythm of their wings like a heartbeat he could count on. People crossed the street when he muttered, when his words tangled into threads no one else could follow. But the pigeons stayed. They cocked their heads as if they understood, as if they'd been waiting.

The city, though—that was a liar. Buildings shifted overnight. Crosswalks led nowhere. Streetlights blinked in patterns he half-recognized, like Morse code filtered through static. He remembered things that weren't there, forgot things that were. Sometimes he thought the city was breathing, inhaling him, exhaling a version that didn't fit.

Jeremiah Moon

He tried to write it down. Not maps exactly—he wasn't Maps Morales, though he knew the man, once, from a shelter kitchen where soup burned too thin. Dominic's notebook was filled with lists. Words. Half-sentences. Numbers that meant something at the time but unraveled when he read them again.

$\nabla//\psi$ appeared most often.
Sometimes carved into margins. Sometimes written in his sleep.
He didn't remember learning the symbol. He only remembered the way it made his chest tighten, like seeing a shadow where no one stood.

The intake worker at Edgewater Shelter told him the notebook was "symptomatic." She didn't ask what of.

The night Ava came, he was already half-gone.

Rain had turned the sidewalk into a mirror, neon signs swimming in puddles. He crouched under the overhang, pen out of ink, notebook pages damp, pigeons clustered close for warmth. He remembered her voice first—steady, quick, the way reporters talked when they wanted you to trust them. "Name?" she asked gently, her handwriting looping across the form.

"Parr," he muttered. "Or Dominic. Depends which day."

She didn't flinch. Most did. Her pen didn't pause.

"Age?"

He had to think. Numbers slipped, years collided. "Forty. Or thirty-eight. I... don't know anymore."

The Invisible People

Her eyes flickered—not pity, not disbelief, something else. Recognition? He wanted to ask if she felt it too, if the world had slipped for her, but the words tangled in his throat.

She guided him through the questions, patient even when his answers broke apart. Last job? Software engineer. Maybe. Last address? A condo near the water, except he couldn't remember the street, only that the windows rattled when the tide was high. Medical conditions? "Just the edits," he whispered, then laughed too loud, scaring the pigeons.

"Edits?" she pressed, and for a moment he saw curiosity burn in her eyes. Not dismissal. Not the glazed-over stare of the caseworkers. But interest, sharp and alive.

He wanted to tell her everything. About the static in the walls, the signs that blinked messages only he could read, the way the pigeons sometimes spoke in her voice. But the words clumped together, thick, heavy, nonsensical. By the time he blinked, she had already moved on to the blood type section, her pen scratching steady, efficient.

"O negative," he said automatically, and she wrote it down without question. He remembered the way her hair caught the fluorescent light, the ink stain on her thumb, the steadiness of her presence. A tether. A ghost.

And then it blurred.

He woke on the cot hours later, the form tucked into his file, Ava gone. He remembered her. Then he didn't. Then he did again, but wrong—her voice replaced by static, her name erased.

Jeremiah Moon

The pigeons circled above the shelter roof that morning, wings flashing silver in the dawn. They whispered, or maybe he only imagined it:

You won't remember.

He scratched the symbol $\nabla//\psi$ into the underside of his cot with a spoon. Proof for later. Something to find when memory slipped.

The weeks blurred. Soup lines. Shelter floors. The smell of bleach and mildew. He thought he saw Ava again once, across the street near Clematis, her hair tied back, a press badge clipped to her jacket. He tried to wave, but his hand felt too heavy, his body stuck in tar. She didn't see him. Or she did, and her eyes slid past, like everyone else's.

That was when the pigeons started bringing him things. A cigarette butt. A paper clip. Once, a photo—creased, water-damaged, showing a group of people he didn't recognize. Except one. A young man, eyes shadowed, sketchbook in hand. Maps Morales. Dominic stared until the image blurred, until his eyes burned. By the next morning, the photo was gone, carried off or erased.

The pigeons cooed at him from the roof.
Anchor. Drift. Replace.
Words that weren't words.

Winter bit harder that year. He lost two toes to frostbite, the skin gray, the pain sharp enough to keep him awake. The clinic wrapped his foot, gave him antibiotics. He told them about the edits, about the city rearranging itself, about the pigeons that knew more than

51

the people. They wrote "paranoid delusions" in his file, neat handwriting he couldn't erase no matter how he scratched at the page.

But one nurse—short hair, clipped tone—paused when he muttered about $\nabla//\psi$. She glanced at her tablet, frowned, then smiled too quickly. "You'll be fine," she said. Her eyes said something else.

That night, he dreamed of corridors. Endless white halls, flickering lights, doors that opened into rooms he half-recognized: his childhood bedroom, the cubicle where he used to code, the shelter cot, a subway tunnel dripping water. And Ava, standing at the end, holding out her hand. He tried to run, but the floor shifted under him, turning liquid, pulling him down.

When he woke, the pigeons were perched on his cot, silent, watching.

The last clear memory he had before the erasure was the plaza.

He was shouting at the pigeons again, warning them, warning himself. The air stank of radiator fluid, his vape pen empty. People skirted wide around him, muttering. He scrawled $\nabla//\psi$ on the pavement with chalk, certain it would hold the truth. Certain someone would see.

And then—static.

A van. White. No logos. Doors opening too fast. Gloves on his arms, cold against his skin. A voice: "Subject Parr. Drift confirmed."

The pigeons scattered.
Their wings beat like a heart giving out.

Jeremiah Moon

After that, nothing was steady. Fragments. A suit pressed against his skin. A tie too tight. Shoes polished until he could see his face in them. A mirror that smiled back even when he didn't. Phrases whispered into his ears at night: Efficiency. Optimization. Return.

He tried to hold onto Ava, to her steady voice in the shelter, her ink-stained hand filling out his form. He told himself she was real. That she remembered him.

But each day, the memory blurred. Faded. Smoothed. Until all that remained was a hollow echo:

"You must have me confused."

The pigeons never came back after that.

CLEAN RETURNS

8

Ava Chen

She told herself she wasn't looking for him.

It was a nice lie to carry through the morning—small, portable, easy to hold on the walk down Flagler when the breeze off the water felt like refrigerated air and the sky sat too bright over a city that had slept badly. The notebook rode in her tote, warm against her hip as if it remembered more than she did. Pages earlier that day had rearranged themselves into a clean grid, six blocks around City Hall, a lozenge-shaped diagram stamped dead center: Pulse Node. Beneath it, in the same hand that had once been Caleb's and sometimes looked like hers: $\nabla//\psi$.

The symbol didn't throb. It didn't glow. It just waited—same as the plaza.

Jeremiah Moon

She let her feet take her the long way—past the used bookstore with the coughing bell, past the nail salon that changed names too often, past a lamp whose shadow stretched longer than the pole allowed. Twice she stopped, pretending to check her phone when really she needed the world to reassemble itself under her. Twice it did. Mostly.

The night before she'd almost called Dan, her old editor, as if there were a headline to pitch and desk time to beg for. Instead she'd opened a new note in her own words: Not a story. Not yet. Just proof I'm not hallucinating.

The basement of the community center had been her compromise with reality. She'd found Lost Connections at 3 a.m., link buried on a page that shouldn't have been indexed. The map bubble stuttered and then settled over a building she'd biked past a hundred times and never noticed. She went early, on purpose, in case she needed to leave early without being questioned.

The room smelled like old coffee and multipurpose cleaner. Folding chairs in a circle, a corkboard with flyers nobody read: Meal Prep for One. Tenant's Rights. Mindful Walking Tuesdays. She took a chair near the edge. The whiteboard said Share Your Story in a hand that had tried to be cheerful and failed.

"Welcome." The woman who said it looked like a thousand small kindnesses stacked into a person: gray hair pulled back for practicality, a denim shirt with a patch that might have been a seashell, the kind of face that invited confession without asking for it. "I'm Rita. Start where you want. Stop when you need."

They went around, and every voice dressed loss in a different outfit. A man with a ring tan and nervous hands: "My wife, Elena. We had a locksmith change the deadbolt. She still—wasn't there in the morning. Later I saw her in checkout line. She told me I had her mixed up with someone else." His fingers stroked the seam of his jeans like a worry bead. "But she has this thing she does with her jaw when she's trying not to laugh. The woman had it."

A younger woman with tattooed forearms sighed without drama. "Jax. He'd bring me screws and bottle caps like I was a museum. Hated phones. Now he has a start-up and speaks like a TED Talk. His time-line starts last spring. Everything before that 404s."

An older guy with sun-leathered skin cleared his throat three times before his voice worked. "My son, Danny. Scar under his lip from a bike fall at ten. It's in a billboard now. College kid hawking finance in-ternships. He doesn't look like he remembers falling."

Someone made a noise. It might have been Ava.

When it was her turn, the room tilted between two versions of the truth she'd rehearsed and never managed to hold at the same time. She heard herself pick one—locked room, warm tea, sketchbook open to an impossible door—and wished she'd said the other, where officials used the word overdose because a form needed a box checked.

"My brother," she said, and felt the word in her teeth. "Caleb. Three years. I saw him again once. It wasn't him."

Rita nodded as if that made sense. "Sometimes they come back cleaner." She said the word like it tasted wrong. "Anyone seen the sym-bol?" She turned the cap on a dry-erase marker without removing it. "Triangle, double slash, psi?"

Ava had it already on the napkin she'd folded for her coffee. She slid it toward the middle of the circle. It felt like putting a photograph face up.

The balding man flinched. "That was on Elena's phone. It was an app for a day. I clicked it and—nothing. Then it wasn't there."

Ava wrote $\nabla//\psi$ again, darker. "I find it where it shouldn't be," she said. "Receipts. A bus map. On my wall once, like a shadow. Maps— my friend—he called it a tag."

"Who's Maps?" Rita asked, curious, not prying.

"Eddie," Ava said, because saying Eddie was a way to hold him here. "He draws the city like it's a living thing. Or drew."

"You think people are doing this?" the tattooed woman asked the air. "You think someone is… performing a clean on us? Like we're hard drives?"

"I think someone benefits when we forget in the same direction," Rita said gently. "I think some of us don't."

She didn't ask for proof. She didn't ask for sanity. She asked if anyone needed water.

By the end of the hour, Ava had three names circled in her notebook: a receptionist at a walk-in clinic off Belvedere, a "weird little forum" with a thread called memory optimization that went nowhere until it did, and DOMINIC PARR written twice—first from the ring-tanned husband, who remembered him sleeping near the old museum steps and talking to pigeons as if they were coworkers, and then from the tattooed woman, who said "he was one of the first to be… better," in the tone you used when a word was too simple for what it carried.

On the last pass, Rita's eyes found hers. "Whatever you decide to do next," she said, voice lowered, "pay attention to the small changes. Big things get denied. Little things gaslight you." She smiled at the napkin. "If you find more of that, bring it back."

Ava wanted to hug her and also to accuse her of something she couldn't name. Instead she folded the napkin twice and put it back in her pocket. When she stood, the room wobbled, a moment's vertigo like stepping onto an escalator that hadn't started moving yet.

The Invisible People

The plaza was the opposite of that room—clean enough to squeak, marble reflecting a sky that didn't look like it had ever held rain. A banner draped across the City Hall façade like a fresh coat of certainty: NeuroWave Technologies presents FutureLogic '25. A stage had erupted from the steps, all truss and LED, screens looping slogans that could have been about anything. Innovate your neural pathways. Remember what matters. Unlearn the inefficiencies.

She stopped at the perimeter, behind a hedge trimmed too quickly at the corners. The crowd wore lanyards and smiles that started at the cheeks instead of the eyes. Someone handed her a brochure printed on plastic. She didn't take it. The notebook in her bag seemed to shift its weight like a cat noticing birds.

On the big screen, the agenda cycled. She had to blink to be sure the name didn't rearrange itself between frames.

Keynote: Dominic Parr, CEO, Emergent Path Systems.

Her stomach dropped in a familiar way she had never learned to manage. She watched the steps without meaning to breathe. He came out in a navy suit that conceded nothing—waist subtle, shoulders correct, shoes that made a sound when they decided to. A headset sat at his mouth as if he'd been born with it. For half a second the light caught his face at an angle she remembered: chapped lips, the red chafe where a scarf had been too tight last winter, eyes that used to flicker like neon deciding whether to stay on. Then the angle shifted and all of that vanished under polish.

"Cognitive restructuring," he said, warm in the way a recorded message at a small-town airport is warm, "is an old idea with a new scale. We have legacy habits that serve us until they don't. We can optimize without losing who we are."

A murmur of agreement. A few phones lifted.

Ava stepped closer.

He moved like the building had been made for him—enough space in each gesture, a calibrated pause before each slide. The screen behind him offered diagrams that pretended to be simple: a tangle of noise smoothed into a single braided line; a brain made of dots, some of them red until they weren't; a list of words that formed a staircase if you squinted just right.

Sometimes her eyes played a trick. For a frame too brief to trust, pigeons wheeled around him like a crown of small gods, heads bobbing in time to a man scattering crumbs from a paper bag. When she refocused, he was pointing at a minimal slide titled PHASE PROTOCOL. In the bottom right corner, tiny, faint, there and gone—$\nabla//\psi$.

She lowered her head as if writing. Her thumb hit the camera from inside her tote. One picture mid-syllable. One when he exhaled. One of the slide's corner that wasn't supposed to matter. The phone accepted them. She didn't check.

"We resist change not because we fear improvement," he said as the applause told him this was the place for a soundbite, "but because memory and identity are intertwined. Remembering becomes a habit. Sometimes the habit isn't serving us. We can rewrite—"

The word didn't feel like a mistake until it had already left his mouth. He covered it efficiently. "—retune."

The applause caught, then continued.

After, people in jackets with logos she didn't recognize and haircuts she absolutely did formed a line for nothing specific. He stepped off to the side, flanked but not guarded. Efficiency wrote itself through his posture. She waited for someone to claim him, to whisk him into a black SUV, to deny her the chance to do what she'd promised herself she wasn't here to do.

"Dominic," she said.

He turned exactly as if he turned whenever anyone said his name and calculated the response. His eyes were a color you couldn't ask a screen to get right. They held hers for as long as courtesy required. "Yes?"

"You remember me."

It was a statement that made her nauseous to hear herself say. He frowned a little in a way you'd learn in a class. "Should I?"

"Clinic intake," she said. "Edgewater. Winter, two years ago. Frostbite that ended up not being frostbite. You had a cut under your ring finger. O negative. You told me that like it was a joke." Her voice wobbled between claims, tapping the table of memory for a glass she couldn't see. "You... talked to the pigeons because no one else was talking to you."

His smile did an impressive job at being both apologetic and noncommittal. "That doesn't sound like me."

It did, and then it didn't. Her heart had a new beat. She couldn't tell if it was a glitch in the room or her.

"I brought you tea," she said, too fast. "You said it tasted like batteries."

"Ma'am," he said softly, and any argument that wants to be called unreasonable hears that word with a wince. "I was a lot of things. I've moved on. I'm grateful to anyone who helped me then, truly. I'm not him now."

"I don't think that's how being a person works."

For a fraction—less than a blink—something sad crossed his face like a ripple that doesn't want to be a wave. If she'd wanted to be kinder, she could have left it alone. If she'd wanted to be safe, she would have left already.

"You're better," she said, and hated how the word scraped. "You're—clean."

He didn't flinch. He had practiced not flinching. "I'm lucky," he said. "Not everyone gets a second chance."

The people with logos moved in politely, the way ants reorganize themselves when a shoe interrupts their plan. "We're late," someone said to no one. He nodded at Ava as if closing a tab. "Thank you for coming."

He went down the escalator with hands not touching the rail. The sound of his soles on the treads was perfect metronome. She stood there until the lanyards stopped orbiting. Until the screen cycled to sponsors. Until the pigeons forgot they were extras.

Her hands were cold. The phone felt hot. She took it out and checked the photos before she could come up with a reason not to. They were there: a face in profile that used to bark at birds, a suit that could read a boardroom into applause, the lower right of a slide with tiny pixels that weren't an accident. She backed them up to a cloud she didn't trust and emailed them to herself at three accounts she never checked.

On the walk to the café she tried to think of language that didn't collapse under the weight of what she wanted to say. Dominant narrative. Algorithmic memory. Curators. The word felt invented and inevitable. She didn't write it down.

At the counter, Donnie watched her over a stack of cups like he was picking a moment. "You good?" he asked when the line thinned. His tone could go either way.

"I just watched a man I used to wipe battery tea off of give a talk about turning people into better versions of themselves."

Donnie leaned his hip against the espresso machine. "Like those glow-up videos where they shave and buy one shirt."

61

"Something like that."

He made her a coffee she didn't ask for, the result of affectionate repetition. He didn't say they move on; that was earlier, different morning, different doubt. He said, "Be careful," which was the weapon you give someone when they are going to walk into a fight without you.

Back home, the apartment had the wrong temperature by two degrees. She set her tote down carefully as if it held something alive. The notebook opened to wherever it wanted to be. Today that was a transit map rendered so clean it felt like a threat. A circle around City Hall. A thin line connecting it to nowhere, labeled PHASE: OPEN.

She turned a page. Her hand didn't do it. The paper whispered anyway. A list spilled out that looked like it had been written by more than one person: CLINIC VOL. — KARA; BUS CAM, NORTH; BEN TRUSS (PUBLIC RECORDS); DOMINIC PARR. The last was circled, the circle darker than the others, like a bruise.

Her phone pinged with an email to herself that she recognized by subject line alone. Attached: three photos from the plaza, time stamps and geotags intact. She opened the one of the slide corner and zoomed until pixels were squares. $\nabla//\psi$ lived there, as responsible as a watermark.

She started a message to Rita and stopped. She wrote it again. Need to talk about returns. I have something. She added, It's not proof yet. She deleted the last sentence because she hated it. Sent.

The reply came too fast to have been typed. Tomorrow. Bring whatever you can that survived. —R

She paced from sink to couch to door and back. The second pass she imagined she was counting breaths. The fourth she realized she was counting edits: the scuff on the third stair was gone; the fridge hum shifted frequency when she looked away from it; the streetlight outside hadn't buzzed in hours and should have. Her nails left little crescents in her palms. Somewhere between the door and the couch, the phone blinked with a notification from nothing. For one breath the screen held text that wasn't a message: ANCHOR OBSERVED. NULL-CLASS. Then it was the lock screen again.

She sat. She didn't know when she had started shaking. The notebook obligingly slid to a blank page, except it wasn't blank; faint letters rose into view the way a bruise blooms.

NEXT: Subject Parr active. Instability window: 72 hours.

Nothing in her knew what the sentence wanted. The only thing that mattered in its grammar was the word window. They closed. You missed them. You cracked them open with your fingers and they cut you.

The sound she made wasn't a laugh and wasn't not. She took her pen and wrote in large, sloppy letters that took faith to form: I REMEMBER YOU.

Then smaller, below it, because she couldn't help bargaining with her own certainty: For now.

She texted Rita one more line she wasn't sure she should send: If they erase him, I still have him. Right?

The dots blinked. Stopped. Blinked.

Bring two copies, Rita wrote. And don't walk home the same way twice.

CROSSINGS

9

Malik Rios (Core Thread)

Malik stood at Mercer and 12th.

The traffic signal blinked red—blue—red.

Not a malfunction. A warning.

Its rhythm pulsed like a heartbeat out of sync with the city's breath.

The air carried static. Heavy.

As if West Palm's veins were wired and live, humming beneath the skin.

He adjusted his coat collar. Fingers brushed the dead recorder hidden beneath the lapel. Tape jammed years ago. Habit kept it close.

He didn't need it anymore.

He was the tape now.

His head played back what no one else could hear—loops of sound, not static but breathing. Human. Like someone remembering they once stood here, on this corner, in this version of the city.

He pulled a folded page from his pocket. Ink blurred at the crease. Ava's scrawl, rushed:

Don't trust the man in the coat. Even if it's you.

Not his words.

But they carried his urgency.

A warning from a woman he hadn't met in this loop. Not yet.

Still—he remembered her.

Coffee shop that didn't exist.

Half a conversation.

Silence the loop forgot to fill.

Ava remembered differently.

Her notebook anchored her.

He remembered too much—fragments crowding his skull like static.

He stepped into the crosswalk. The moment his boot touched curb, the sidewalk flickered.

People lagged half a beat behind their shadows.

A child's jump-rope reset mid-hop.

A bird rewound three wingbeats before catching up.

The world smoothed.

But the wrongness stayed. Ozone sharp.

Seen too long, he thought. *Anchor bleed.*

His hand patted the coat. Badge humming like a tuning fork. Not an ID. A reminder. A tether.

A man on a bench stared too directly. For a flicker, Malik's own jawline stared back—then collapsed into a stranger.

Variants. Sloppy.

The pull in his chest deepened. A loop nearby. Unstable. Ava's, maybe. Or another's.

The Invisible People

He followed it, weaving through streets bent by edits. Corners sharper than they should be. Distances stretched, then shortened.

An alley pulled him in. Narrow. Angles wrong. The geometry off, like a draft sketched too quickly. The air heavy with scorched metal.

At the far end—a woman in a pale coat. Her outline shimmered, glitching. Not Ava. Close. Almost.

She turned. Eyes doubled, out of sync.

"You shouldn't be here," she said. Voice layered, two tracks at once. "You're not calibrated."

"Neither are you," Malik said. His tone flat. Steady.

"I'm only watching."

"Then watch this."

He drew the badge. Its shimmer pulsed—heartbeat, memory. The alley buckled. Bricks bent, shadows snapped back into place.

Her face fractured—two, then three, then gone. The voice lagged half a second before silence.

She vanished. Only the hum remained.

The geometry straightened. Reality clicked into alignment, too neat.

Malik exhaled. Breath visible in air that wasn't cold.

She's close, he thought. *They're watching her again.*

He tapped the badge against his palm. Bones rattled. For a blink, another scene bled in—a hospital corridor. A glass wall. Ava's hand against it. Eyes pleading through the barrier. Then gone.

He pulled his coat tight. The city churned back into motion, its pulse still uneven.

Loops always pulled him toward her.

Loops always pulled him back.

He turned toward the light.

Walking into a world that didn't want him to remember.

INTERLUDE: OPERATOR LOG – SUBJECT RIOS

Equinox Initiative // Mirror Watch Subnet – Tier 3 Clearance
Subject Tag: Malik Rios (Core Thread)
Timestamp: $\Delta T+0017:43$ from last Anchor Drift
Status: Active – Unstable

Loop Assessment

- Subject remains tethered to Anchor Chen (Variant 88A).
- Unauthorized retention detected: memory fragments of prior merges persist.
- Reflection latency observed: 0.42s deviation across three surfaces.
- Badge resonance unstable. Should not be carried.

Anomaly Notes

Rios continues to "remember forward." This is not unexpected—he has always carried echoes that belong to no current thread. What *is* unexpected is the strength of retention. He recalls Anchor Chen in loops where contact has not yet occurred. He speaks her words before she delivers them.

This bleed increases his instability rating. It also increases his value.

Risk Summary

- Tether Risk: Elevated. (If Rios collapses, Anchor Chen destabilizes.)
- Replacement Risk: Moderate. (Variants available but calibration incomplete.)
- Containment: Unresolved.

Recommendation debated. Half consensus: remove Rios before drift escalates. Half consensus: preserve until Anchor Chen's instability window closes.

Operator Commentary [Redacted Tier 3]

He was not meant to last this long. Every thread writes him out early. And yet he remains.

Some of us think the loops keep him because he *cares*.
Not efficient. Not predictable. But caring anchors differently.

That may be what makes him dangerous.

[End Log // Subject Rios – Observation Ongoing]

CALEB'S THREAD

10

Caleb Chen

There wasn't a door—not anymore—just a wall of static pretending to be silence, its hum vibrating in Caleb's bones like a machine that had forgotten how to stop. He stood before it, palm pressed against nothing, the surface warm, pulsing, as if the air itself had a heartbeat. The corridor behind him throbbed, a sick machine lurching without rhythm, its walls flickering like old projector film, frames stuttering, burning, rewinding. Time didn't behave here—it didn't flow, it lurched, a broken reel of moments that refused to align. His mind insisted Ava had vanished seconds ago, her laughter still echoing, but another part whispered it had been forever, a grief so heavy it bent his spine. The more he tried to pin it down, the more it slipped, like water spilling through cupped hands, leaving only the ache of its absence.

Jeremiah Moon

The walls shifted, showing fragments of his apartment: dirty dishes stacked in the sink, coffee going cold, the window unit rattling against Florida's relentless heat. Then Ava, laughing, her shoulders shaking in a way no photograph could capture, a real laugh from a time when they were whole. Once, they showed him—hospital gown, a number tattooed under his collarbone, eyes hollow, wrong, staring from a version he didn't recognize. He stopped watching after that, his stomach twisting, the air tasting metallic, sharp at the back of his throat, like blood or burned circuits.

He moved carefully, each step deliberate, like walking across a frozen lake he couldn't see, the corridor's pulse unsteady beneath his boots. Every few paces, he whispered Ava's name, not expecting an answer, needing the ritual, the word a tether to something beyond this place, a string tied to his ribs, pulling him forward. Sometimes the corridor answered—not with her voice, but with voices shaped like hers: once in fluent French, calling him *Doctor*, warm, intimate, as if she trusted him; another time screaming in a language he didn't know, her reflection bleeding against a shattered window; once whispering a prayer, soft, fading before he could catch it. He carved these fragments into his sleeve with a stub of broken graphite, the ink dissolving, but the grooves remained, memory pressed into cloth, a map of loss that refused to fade.

He remembered Ava as the girl who sat with him during thunderstorms, inventing stories until thunder became applause, her voice a light in the dark. Other times, she was a stranger in a police station, signing a missing-person report with steady hands, eyes empty. Both were real, both hers, but not the same her. Which Caleb was he? The overdose in a halfway house, filed away in a municipal archive? The one who vanished, door locked, tea warm? Or another, never meant to last? The question hung, heavy as the static, a weight he couldn't shake.

The Invisible People

The passage bent, not turned—*bent*, sharper than geometry allowed, curving into itself, twisting his stomach. He pressed forward, boots squeaking on linoleum that wasn't there moments ago. There she was—Ava, or something shaped like her, standing before a mirror shimmering like oil on water, shoulders relaxed, hands loose. She turned, smiling, but it wasn't Ava's smile—too practiced, too symmetrical, a copy polished until nothing imperfect remained. "You're not supposed to be here," she said, her voice rippling, layered, as if another spoke beneath it, a chorus of wrongness.

Caleb stepped back, pulse pounding. "Neither are you," he said, his voice steady despite the tremor in his chest.

The mirror quivered, light folding and unfolding. Visions flickered: Malik falling, badge slipping from his coat, grief sharp as a blade; Maps sprinting down a fractured street, notebook pages scattering like wings; Zara screaming into a microphone, voice tearing her throat raw, feed cutting to silence. Caleb looked away, eyes stinging, the images burning into his mind.

"This corridor doesn't loop," the false Ava said. "It folds. It forgets. Choose what you remember before it chooses for you."

He pulled the ruined notebook from his pocket—blank pages, spine warped, once Ava's, now just an anchor. "I want Ava," he said, voice breaking.

She laughed, hollow as a ringtone. "Which one?"

The mirror split. Twelve Avas stepped forward—one crying, one furious, one with a knife, one holding a child, one refusing his gaze, one smiling too brightly, one already leaving. The sight stole his breath, his heart a trapped thing.

Caleb closed the notebook, pressed it to his chest, and whispered, "The one who stayed."

Jeremiah Moon

The corridor cracked—not collapsed, but *shattered*, like glass under pressure. He fell through, hitting asphalt hard enough to bruise, rain splattering his face, cool, real, smelling of wet concrete, gasoline, bad plumbing. The world blurred—headlights smeared, neon signs humming too bright, their buzz a warning. The rain fell in code: five drops, pause, five drops, pause. A streetlight stayed green too long, a siren wailed without fading, looping endlessly.

Caleb staggered upright, knees aching, palms stinging. The notebook was gone, but in his pocket—a damp, creased napkin, Ava's scrawl: *Find the one who remembers. Tell her I saw it too.* His hand trembled, chest burning. He didn't know which Caleb he was—overdose, disappeared, or something else. But he knew she was out there. And she remembered.

NOTES FROM THE LOST

11

Ava Chen

The notebook sat on her kitchen table like it was waiting for her. Not inert. Not forgotten. Waiting. Ava had walked past it half a dozen times since midnight, each pass convincing herself she wouldn't look. Yet each time, she swore the top page was different—pencil strokes sharper, a smudge in the margin that hadn't been there before. Maybe it was light, maybe fatigue. Or maybe it was her. She was starting to accept that she was the weaker variable, easier to shift than the world around her.

At 3:12 a.m., barefoot, restless, she gave in. "Okay," she whispered, voice trembling against the apartment's silence. "Okay." The chair creaked under her weight as she sat. She opened the notebook.

Symbols filled the first page—glyphs that weren't words, coordinates stacked like a machine's attempt at poetry. She traced one with her fingertip. Static pricked up her arm, quick and sharp, gone before she could name it. Imagination, she told herself. But the sensation lingered.

She turned the page. This time the lines settled into a map: 7th and Halsey, the Redhaven Shelter marked at the center. The name alone pressed on her chest. Disinfectant and burnt soup clung to memory. Caleb had stayed there once—two nights, maybe three—during a rare clean spell. She'd dropped off socks, left before he asked her to stay. Guilt walked out with her and never stopped following.

The map's circle was thick, red, insistent. Beneath it, three words:

Still there. Almost.

"Almost?" she murmured, voice catching. Rita's warning from the support circle echoed back: *A lot of our stories start at Redhaven. People check in, but some never check out.*

She snapped the notebook shut, heart thudding. When she reopened it, the page hadn't shifted. The circle was still there. The words still waited. She grabbed her keys and a flashlight. Sweat-stained shirt, tangled hair—the city didn't care.

Fog clung to the streets, thick as grief. Sodium lamps buzzed, their light faltering in sync with her pulse. The rideshare driver glanced at her in the mirror.

"That area's rough at night," he said. "You sure?"

"I'm sure." The words came steady, though they didn't feel like hers. The notebook warmed in her lap, like an animal pretending to sleep.

Redhaven crouched at the corner, windows boarded, fence rusted through. Layers of tags clashed in unreadable argument, color bleeding into fog. Ava slipped through a gap, the tape at the gate crumbling in her fingers—old, brittle, cosmetic.

Inside, the air smelled of wet paper and old smoke. Her flashlight beam caught a sign above the front desk: **REHABILITATION IS A RIGHT.** Half the letters dangled by single nails, trembling in the draft.

"Hello?" she said before she could stop herself.

The building answered with a click deep in the ducts, sharp as a tongue snapping shut.

She moved through rooms slowly. Charred couches. A bulletin board crowded with flyer ghosts. PSA posters defaced, slogans buried under spray paint. The silence wasn't silence—it creaked like lungs straining to breathe.

The intake office was cleaner. Desk intact. A half-melted nameplate. A mug fossilized with rings of coffee. She tugged open a drawer. Intake forms—rubber-banded, paper curling at the edges. *Transient. Unhoused. Mental health referral.* Ink that looked wrong, like it had hesitated before drying.

Then she saw it: **Caleb Chen.** Dated 2022.

Her breath caught. Symptoms listed: *disorientation, memory lapses.* Below, a note in tidy, detached script: *Referred to Equinox Pilot Program.*

The two endings of Caleb's story—overdose, locked apartment—clashed in her chest. And now a third. She took photos, then folded the form carefully, sliding it into her jacket pocket, palm pressing over it as if to keep it from dissolving.

A glint behind the filing cabinet caught her light. She crouched and tugged out a manila folder, tabbed in Sharpie: **MAPS.** Her throat tightened. Inside: empty. Except for one sticky note, glue degraded to grease. *You weren't supposed to find this either.*

The air thickened. The building seemed to inhale.

Her beam swept the wall. There—scratched in stubborn charcoal: $\nabla//\psi$.

She pressed her palm against it. Cold. Tingling static traced her fingers. Dust stirred—not randomly, but in a line, faint footprints leading down the hall. Maps's shuffle. His stubborn gait.

She followed. Kitchen door sagging, tiles blackened. Bathroom mirror cracked like a spiderweb frozen mid-shatter. Therapy office with two chairs facing like adversaries. The prints ended at a blank wall, dust cut into a right angle: the shadow of a doorway without a door.

The notebook buzzed faintly in her hand. She opened it. One sentence sprawled across the page: **They erased the door, but not the memory.**

Her breath fogged. Memory surged—Caleb at Redhaven, nailbeds raw, fidgeting with a styrofoam cup. *Coffee?* he'd asked. *I'm late,* she'd said, walking away, trusting the city's seal. Another flash—her voice, tinny, impatient: *We'll talk tomorrow.* Guilt twisted in her gut. She couldn't tell if it was her memory, or something the notebook had written into her.

Noise scraped the shelter's bones—vents whispering, pipes knocking like knuckles on hollow doors.

On the desk, a single pigeon feather lay against the wood. Out of place. Dominic Parr flickered in her thoughts—bread crumbs scattered for pigeons in a plaza too clean.

Near the switch plate, two shallow letters carved into paint: **MR.**

Her stomach flipped. *Malik Rios?* Common initials, she lied to herself. The lie didn't stick.

The sign overhead flickered—**REHABILITATION IS A RIGHT.** Brightened once. Dimmed. Fell silent.

Outside, fog pressed cool fingers against her skin. Streetlights lingered on green too long. A pedestrian signal flashed WALK and DON'T WALK at once.

She texted Rita: *Found something at Redhaven. Caleb's intake. Equinox mentioned. Sending photo.* The message sent. No read receipt.

At home, she switched on every light. The glow flooded her apartment, but it didn't bring safety. She named objects aloud—"Sink. Tile. Postcard. Mug."—the old grounding exercise her therapist had given her. Her eyes caught the postcard. St. Augustine lighthouse. Caleb's note: *Wish you were here.* It read like a taunt now.

Her phone buzzed: **BLOCKED ID.**

She answered. "Hello?"

A woman's voice, precise, clipped: "Ms. Chen. Your presence at Redhaven has been logged."

Her stomach iced. "Who is this?"

"You are monitored for irregularities."

"What does that mean?"

"Return to routine," the voice said. "Further deviation may result in reclassification."

"To what?"

A pause. Not thought—lag.

Then, almost kind: "You are not alone. That is the problem."

Jeremiah Moon

The line went dead.

Ava lowered the phone slowly, its weight burning in her hand.

The fridge hummed. The clock ticked. The vent rattled. Beneath it all, something deeper pulsed.

On the table, the notebook shivered once, then stilled—like a sleeper adjusting.

Tomorrow she would meet Rita, bring the form, call it what it was.

Tonight she stood in the kitchen, lights blazing, city pressing at her windows.

Her whisper barely reached the air: "How many got that call before they vanished?"

The ducts clicked in reply. Sharp. Final.

And the notebook's edges pulsed once more, as if listening.

INTERLUDE: OPERATOR DEBRIEF –
THE MORALES INTERFERENCE

Operator Record: Classified Debrief // Tier 5 Clearance – Eye-Only

Subject: Elias "Maps" Morales
Thread Status: Contaminated
Echo Class: Civilian-Adjacent / Observer Drift-Aware
Deviation Report: Incident Redline–17B

Preface – Extract from Subject Journal (Recovered Fragment)
"You asked me to stop drawing them.
But the corridors don't stop walking through me."

Incident Overview

ΔT–03:04 local drift time – Subject Morales submitted a sketch to the Network.

- Drawing was not requested.
- Not prompted.
- Timestamp predated corridor manifestation at 12th and Carmine by **three minutes**.

This is the **third confirmed instance of precognitive illustration.**

Analyst Note: Subject interprets sketches as "dream residuals." Predictive capacity remains unconscious. Despite multiple resets, the cognitive link persists. Memory loops remain fragmented but retain **emotional resonance signatures** beyond allowable drift thresholds. Emotional tethering appears resistant to standard suppression.

Anomaly Tags

- **Predictive Rendering Without Loop Trigger**
- **Ava Chen imprint visible in corner signature (ink bleed overlapping drift glyphs)**
- **Caleb Chen distortion node visible as marked absence in composition**
- **Corridor bleed geometry: 97.6% accuracy (within 2.4% drift tolerance)**

- **Seed Echo Hypothesis: Subject consciousness demonstrating "forward bleed" consistent with Quantum Seed drift**

Operator Commentary – Unattributed

"He isn't Echo-Class. He's something older. Something outside protocol."

"His mind holds corridors like others hold scent memories."

"The question isn't why he draws them.

The question is: *who is asking him to?*"

Incident Redline–17B Summary
- Corridor manifestation triggered without scheduled calibration.
- One Observer lost (Tier 2).
- Three Surveillance Nodes collapsed before reconstitution.
- Subject Morales' sketch matched breach geometry with near-total fidelity.
- Causality indeterminate: **Did he predict the corridor, or did the corridor use him to pre-exist?**

Recommended Action
- Do not initiate rewrite.

- Morales remains too valuable as a passive leak.
- Permit sketches to continue; monitor bleedthrough frequency.
- Limit external interference — Subject fear responses generate more accurate glyph renderings.
- Containment remains optional. Termination, if ordered, must be **clean**.

Addendum – Curator Cell Echo-Theta Directive

Morales is to remain unoptimized.
Let him remember just enough to be afraid.
Fear is calibration.

Memo Forwarded: Curator Cell Echo-Theta
Access Lock: Tether Surveillance Only
End Transmission

INTERLUDE: ECHO LOG - SUBJECT 8829

Classified: INTERNAL—EQUINOX DATASTREAM
Audio Recovered: Subject 8829
Origin: White Corridor // Bay 14B
Status: Unstable
Access Level: Restricted // Ψ-13
Timestamp: ΔT–044:19 from Drift Initiation
Corruption Rating: 37% (increasing)

[BEGIN TRANSCRIPT – CONTINUED]

It's not just the bird now.

Last night, the mirror turned on before I touched it. Not the light—the glass.

Jeremiah Moon

It shimmered. Not reflection, not electricity. More like breath across water. The surface pulled inward as though it wanted me closer.

I leaned in.

Something blinked from the other side.

Not me.

The eyes were off by half a second. When they caught up, the expression wasn't one I'd made.

They tell me it's dreaming. Reintegration feedback. "Residual pattern artifacts," they call it. Harmless echo.

But I remember my real dreams. The ones from before the white rooms. Before optimization.

I used to dream of drowning in steam vents. Of my teeth falling out in snow. Of pigeons on fire escapes, heads turning together like they were listening for instructions.

Now I dream in clean lines. Vector graphics. Wireframes repeating on loop.

When I wake, I'm already tired. Like I've been working all night in someone else's body.

Sometimes I catch myself narrating out loud. "Subject 8829 is brushing his teeth. Subject 8829 is compliant."

The Invisible People

Who am I reporting to?

[Glitch detected – audio delay corrected]

There's a hallway outside my unit that doesn't exist on the floor plan.

Three doors. No numbers.

They hum.

I walked past one yesterday. Heard my own voice inside. But I wasn't speaking. I held my breath. Put my ear to the metal. Heard a woman crying. My name. My real name. I think.

I knocked.

Nothing.

When I looked again, the hallway was gone.

[Pause – static interference // 12.6s]

This morning my reflection didn't blink.

I waited. Tried again.

Still nothing.

Jeremiah Moon

He's waiting.
Or maybe I am.

[Deep breath – subject unstable]

I miss the stairwell behind the dry cleaner. The rats. The smell of bleach that never covered the mildew. The sunlight hitting the concrete at exactly 6:42 a.m.

That world was broken.

But it was mine.

This one? This one fits too well.

That's how you know it's a lie.

[END OF RECORDING – SIGNAL DEGRADED]

ANALYST NOTES

- Subject demonstrates **loop narration** (third-person self-surveillance).
- Mirror anomalies increasing in duration. Possible **drift entity reflection**.
- Dream vectors show overlap with Morales-Style Predictive Rendering (vectorized loops).
- Pigeon imagery persistent. Cross-reference with **Parr (Dominic)** pre-optimization signatures.

- Corridor memory bleed matches $\nabla//\psi$ glyph activity (high risk).

PRIORITY STATUS
- File tagged: **DRIFT LEVEL 3**
- Retain for observation. Further optimization not recommended.
- Subject at risk of "forward bleed" into Anchor Chen (Variant 88A).

Observer Intersection Detected: CHEN, AVA

Flagged for escalation // Tier 5 Review Pending

ECHO LOG

SUBJECT ID: 8829

RECORD DATE
00/■■/■■■

MEM DATA

 CORRUPTED

EVENT TAG
ECHO / GLITCH-CLASS 3 / INTERFERENCE

RECOVERY PROTOCOL
PARTIAL RECONSTRUCTION – ARCHIVE CORRIDOR

⚠ Memory fragment has experienced critical
data loss. Reconstruction buffer allocated.
Core memory artifacts may appear altered.

PARTIAL RECONSTRUCTION OUTPUT

...I DIED DOWN HERE...

44

REVERSAL DRAFT

12

Caleb Chen (Thread Unknown)

The first time Caleb saw the red door, it wasn't there—not in the way doors exist, solid and certain, but as a memory bleeding backward into waking, a shape pressed into absence, tugging at the edges of language like déjà vu inverted. The corridor leading to it stretched unnaturally long, as if it had inhaled and refused to exhale, its walls bowing inward, pulsing faintly, alive with a rhythm that didn't match his own. Each footstep landed muted, not soft but wrong, as if the floor had forgotten how to echo, swallowing sound into a void that watched him back. The air was thick, heavy with static, tasting of metal and something sharper, like regret burned into ozone.

His pockets were empty—no notebook, no anchor, only the shard, a sliver of mirror glass tucked in his sleeve, sharp enough to cut, fragile enough to crumble. It pressed against his pulse, cold and insistent, a relic from a place where Ava's face had once looked back through broken silver. He told himself it was a weapon, a tool to carve through this place, but it felt like a curse, an edge that might split him open if he pressed too hard. His fingers twitched, brushing the shard, and a jolt of cold pricked his skin, as if it recognized him before he recognized himself.

Halfway down the corridor, a panel stuttered to life, glyphs flickering across its surface in faint red:

MERGE RESTRICTION IN PLACE // SUBJECT: DEFERRED.

The words pulsed once, twice, then dimmed, leaving a suggestion of heat, a warning that lingered in his teeth. He didn't know how long he'd been here—minutes, hours, years, time lurching like a broken machine. His mind screamed Ava had vanished seconds ago, her laughter echoing, but another part whispered it had been forever, a grief so heavy it bent his spine. The red door waited at the corridor's end, not painted but remembered red, as if his mind colored it to hold it real. The air around its frame vibrated, tension in a wire, and when he pressed his palm against it, warmth spread, not from the wood but from memory, a pulse that wasn't his.

He moved closer—and the corridor itself spoke.

Not words, not exactly, but a layering of voices pulled forward through time:

Ava's whisper, brittle with exhaustion—"You were never supposed to see this far."

Maps's gravel-rough laugh, overlapping—"Paper doesn't lie to itself."

Malik's steady baritone, fractured by static—"Don't trust the man in the coat. Even if it's you."

The Invisible People

The voices braided, discordant, until the air thickened with pressure. Caleb's knees buckled, his hands slamming the wall to stay upright. He wanted to cover his ears, but the sound wasn't in his ears—it was in his ribs, his teeth, his pulse. They weren't just voices; they were memories unmoored, fragments bleeding through from lives he hadn't lived but still carried.

He whispered Ava's name into the static, desperate, like throwing a rope across water. The voices fell silent. The corridor steadied. The door pulsed red again, waiting.

He opened it, stepping into white—not blank-white, but active-white, a silence that hummed with pressure, vibrating in his bones like a scream held back. The room knew him, its geometry alien—smooth corners, seamless surfaces—but the air bent around him, as if it had been waiting, a trap set long before he arrived. Shadows etched themselves into form across the walls, photographs that weren't photographs, negative images scored into light: Ava as a child, hair tangled, holding a library book upside down; Ava in a hospital bed, eyes glazed, drip line feeding her arm; Ava on the Redhaven bridge, wind clawing her coat. Scenes he'd never lived, yet remembered, each a shard of a life he couldn't claim. The glass in his sleeve twitched, cold biting his skin, as if it saw them first. He squeezed his sleeve shut, hiding it from himself. *Not now,* he thought, his voice a whisper in his skull.

The far wall held a mirror, its surface shimmering like oil on water. His breath caught, sharp as a blade. Not his reflection—hers. Ava, alone inside the glass, staring directly at him, her eyes glassy with desperation. For a heartbeat, others layered over her—one laughing, one screaming, one holding a child, one turning away. The images jittered, transparencies stacked carelessly on a lightbox, then smoothed into a single Ava, her gaze piercing. Her lips moved.

"Caleb," she said, her voice rippling, layered, as if spoken from multiple realities.

The shard burned cold against his arm, his throat locking. He knew the rule: *Speak, and the merge begins.* Her hand pressed the glass, breath fogging, a single fingerprint blooming in condensation, curved and exact, a mark that tied her to the Ava who signed his missing-person report. His hand trembled, nearly lifting, the urge to touch her overwhelming. *Ava,* he thought, the name a tether, a prayer. He turned away, the room roaring with silence, vibrating like a taut string. He shut his eyes, counted backward, willing the world to hold still.

He woke, chest heaving, in his apartment, the ceiling cracked and familiar, but wrong, too clean, as if polished overnight. The shard pressed against his wrist, its cold a reminder of where he'd been. On the window beside his bed, condensation spread in a single shape—her fingerprint, exact, a mark no dream could fake. His pulse hammered, the memory not fading but sharpening, a warning carved into reality's skin. Rain splattered outside, falling in coded rhythms—five drops, pause, five drops, pause—like a signal from a place he couldn't name. The streetlight glowed green too long, its hum too steady, a siren looping without end.

Caleb staggered upright, knees aching, palms stinging as if he'd fallen harder than he recalled. The notebook was gone, but in his pocket—a damp, creased napkin, Ava's scrawl: *Find the one who remembers. Tell her I saw it too.* His hand trembled, chest burning with a truth he couldn't place. Was he the overdose Caleb, filed away in a municipal archive? The disappeared Caleb, tea warm, door locked? Or something else, a thread never meant to hold? He didn't know, but one truth anchored him: Ava was out there, remembering, her notebook a lifeline. Some loops were closing, but this one—this one had just opened, a crack in reality's code, pulling him toward her.

REDACTED RETURN

13

Ava

The search bar mocked her, its cursor blinking like a heartbeat out of sync with her own. Every phrase Ava typed—"Dominic Parr," "NeuroWave," "Emergent Path keynote," "FutureLogic Expo"—returned hollow results, SEO sludge written for no one, each page dissolving into sanitized language: *pioneering innovation, synergy with human potential.* Her fingers trembled on the keyboard, the laptop's fan rising and falling as though it, too, was part of the city's conspiracy. She dug deeper—event calendars, city permits, cached press packets—chasing ghosts of data that should have lingered. Nothing. Not even metadata scars. The Expo hadn't just been hidden; it had been scrubbed. Wiped as clean as Maps's alley, as Caleb's locked room.

She slammed the laptop shut. The sound cracked through her apartment, too loud, too final. The silence that followed clung like wet fabric, heavy with static. She tried to steady her breath, but her chest tightened with the memory of Dominic Parr's face, ironed flat into something polished, unrecognizable, refusing to see her. They hadn't erased him. They had overwritten him. *They're rewriting us all,* she thought, the realization a blade pressed to her ribs.

The notebook waited on the kitchen table. It wasn't passive anymore. She could feel its attention, the way it seemed to breathe in the spaces between her own breaths. She sat, reluctant, and opened it.

Gone was Maps's graphite chaos—his fevered layering of grids and alleys. What stared back at her was surgical, almost mechanical: corridors like flowcharts, lettering like a machine testing fonts.

REDAX DETECTED // RETURN INCOMPLETE.

The phrase repeated down the page in perfect spacing, as though stamped by a cold hand. Her stomach soured, the air sharp with ozone. *Not a record. A rewrite,* she thought.

She turned another page. Node designations. A line in cramped script: *Tether pulled before sync — identity lag probable.* Beneath it, in harsh red pencil:

MAPS?

Her fingertip brushed the name. Static pricked her skin, raising gooseflesh. The pages fluttered without her help, landing on an image seared into pulp: Maps hunched on a bench, scarf frayed, head tilted toward a shape blacked out by violent redaction. The edges pulsed faintly, jittering as if the erasure itself were still at work.

Beneath: *He remembered. Then he didn't.*

Her throat closed. She fumbled for the still she'd clipped from the transit feed—Maps stepping off a bus, scarf visible. "How many times did they bring him back?" she whispered. Her eyes caught the number scrawled under the photo: **E9-8829.** The same digits she'd seen embedded in the corrupted audio file last night, the one she deleted three times before it reappeared, whispering of pigeons, stairwells, and prayers.

The notebook snapped shut under her palm, as if to answer.

The apartment felt too small, her thoughts spinning like a server on overheat. She needed a human voice. Not Donnie—too grounded, too unshaken by the edits. Someone who spoke the city's buried language. She pulled her old press drive, the rusted hinge icon blinking alive. Buried folders scrolled past until she found a name: *Ben Truss.* Records analyst, her lifeline during years when the city buried scandals under paperwork.

Her fingers flew. *Hey. Weird one. Got access to incident reports from Edgewater, last 18 months?*

The reply came quicker than it should have. *Depends. What kind?*

Civil detainment. Wellness checks. Maybe anomalous IDs.

Ben: *Weird day for that question.*

Her skin prickled. *Why?*

Ben: *System flagged me this morning. Suppression codes firing on inactive files.*

Her palms went damp. *Redacted?*

Ben: *Beyond redacted. More like the file existed, then got reclassified as never existing.*

She hesitated. Her own memory pulsed wrong—wasn't there a day she and Ben had met at a diner to talk zoning logs? Or had that been someone else? His face blurred when she tried to picture it, details slipping away. *Am I forgetting him? Or is he being rewritten even as we talk?*

She typed anyway: *8829. Can you run it?*

The ellipsis blinked, stopped, blinked again.

Ben: *...You sure?*

Not even a little, she wrote.

Ben: *Two reports. One from 2023. One from... yesterday. 2023's archived, audio corrupted. New one's locked. Ping came from Redhaven. Ava... that place has been dead for years.*

Her chest tightened. *I know.*

Ben: *Whatever you're in, get out.*

She swallowed, fingers shaking. *Too late.*

Ben: *Source?*

She stared at the word until the letters seemed to warp. Then typed: *Me.*

The chat went dark. Logged out. No trace.

She sat frozen, laptop glow flickering against her hands. *If the system can erase people like typos, Ben could be gone by morning. I could be.*

The notebook vibrated—not visibly, but in the air, a weight bending toward her. She opened it again with shaking hands. The photograph was gone. In its place, letters bled upward from the paper, as if surfacing through water:

RE-ENTRY: INCOMPLETE.
SUBJECT: MORALES, EDDIE.
STATUS: DRIFTING.
CLASS: ECHO.
RISK LEVEL: UNSTABLE — OBSERVER CONTACT
CONFIRMED.

Beneath, in clean mechanical type:

PROJECT EQUINOX INITIATIVE. TIER-3 CURATION IN PROGRESS.

Her pulse thudded painfully in her throat, her body syncing with the hum of the fridge, the vent, the clock. The entire room pulsed in rhythm with the page, as though the city itself were leaning closer.

This wasn't Maps's notebook anymore. It was a file. A log. A machine watching her.

She pulled on her jacket, needing air, scanning the room as though the walls were listening. Malik's address surfaced from memory like a buoy. She circled it in ink, her hand trembling. *Déjà vu,* she thought. *I've done this before. I've stood here preparing for a truth I already half-know.*

Her phone buzzed. Rita's reply: *Tomorrow. Bring the notebook. Others need to see it.*

Ava nodded to the empty room, a network coalescing around her grief. Lost Connections was no longer just a circle of voices in a basement. It was becoming resistance.

But when she stepped into the hall, the notebook pulsed faintly in her bag—not ally, not enemy, just a warning. Alive. Waiting to rewrite her.

The light in the corridor flickered once, twice, then steadied. For an instant, she thought she heard Malik's voice in the static—low, urgent, breaking through interference. Then it was gone.

The tether's fr—◆—fraying.
Don't forget—◆—

MALIK (overlapping):
Already?
No, no. Not yet. Not *yet*.

Listen, Ava. I reinforced the echo node at Concord Station. Buried your
name in five separate timelines. Etched it in rail schedules, graffiti tags,
paper receipts. The kind of things they don't bother editing until it's too
late.

It has to hold.
You have to remember me when it matters.

[Silence – 6.2s // Loop Interference Detected]

MALIK (quieter):
If they pull me out—don't anchor on guilt.
That's how they win.

Anchor on truth.
On what still cuts when everything else has been smoothed.

You're the last version that sees the cracks.
The last one still looking through instead of at.

[Final Packet – Corrupted // Words Fragment]

You always fight, Ava.

That's why I—♦ stayed tethered.

That's why—♦♦♦

Transmission Lost

Post Note

Recovered from echo-resonant fragments near Loop Node 14B.

No source terminal located.

Voiceprint match: 96.2% – Rios, Malik.

Classified as **anomalous tether expression**.

Possible evidence of cross-consciousness bleed between Subject 88-A and Operator Rios.

INTERLUDE: ECHO MEMORY – FRAGMENT (ZARA V.)

Recovered from Blackline Artifact Vault // Loop Echo #112-ZV // Status: Residual Drift

"They said I forgot him. But I didn't. I just remembered him in the wrong places."

Subject Overview
Zara V. was not expected to return.
Standard Entangled retention cycle: ≤2 loops.
Zara survived four.

The fifth return produced anomaly: speech in loop-pattern glyphs.

Containment protocols initiated: sedation, memory overwrite, behavioral rewrite.

Residual Anchor
One fragment persisted across all resets:
— Memory of a boy with ink-stained fingers.

Not identified in any verified thread.
Not recorded in official timelines.
Designated: Uncorrelated Entity.

Zara referred to him as **Caleb.**
Not her Caleb.
Not Anchor Chen's Caleb.
A variant echo.

Reported whisper (unverified):

"You're not wrong. Just early."

Artifact Recovery
In white-room observation, Zara wrote with invisible ink.
Visual inspection: null.
Spectral analysis under ultraviolet drift light revealed text:

"The corridors don't forget. They reflect."
"One Ava breaks. Another repeats."
"But the third? The third remembers for all of them."
"She hasn't arrived yet. But she's already watching."

Termination of Speech Output
Post-incident, Zara ceased verbal communication.
Observed state: wide-eyed, unblinking.
Designation updated: Echo – Dormant.

Operator Addendum
Subject sketch recovered: Elias "Maps" Morales produced visual rendering of Zara from memory.

Analyst Note: likeness consistent with witness accounts—expression frozen mid-sentence, as if attempting to deliver a warning seconds before signal collapse.

[End Fragment // Status archived under Drift-Theta protocols]

SPLIT FREQUENCY

14

Ava Chen (Drift-Cusp)

The train platform was too quiet. Not empty, but wrong—a silence that pressed against Ava's skin like static, heavy with the weight of something unseen.

People stood in tidy rows, spines straight, eyes forward, breathing synced to an invisible metronome that ticked in a rhythm she couldn't hear. No chatter. No coughs. No one adjusting a scarf or rubbing a wrist. Even the shuffles of shoes on tile came in matched pairs, as if the crowd had rehearsed the act of waiting, their movements choreographed by a hand she couldn't name.

Ava stood among them, the notebook pressed to her ribs like a shield to keep her bones in place. Its warmth pulsed through her jacket, a reminder of Maps's erased face and Caleb's fractured thread.

106

Her phone buzzed. The lock screen was blank, time frozen at 00:00:00. She blinked, checked again. Still 00:00:00. As if time had surrendered to symmetry, refusing to move forward.

The fluorescent lights hummed in staggered thirds, an off-key drone that made her jaw ache. The air was thick with ozone, hot metal, wet concrete, a scent that clawed at her senses.

Down the tunnel, the rails sang low, uncommitted, as if a train considered arriving but thought better of it.

The intercom crackled overhead, tinny and wrong: "This is the last train to Reconciliation. All deviations, please exit now."

No one moved. Ava didn't either. The word *Reconciliation* stuck like a splinter. With what? With whom? The question burned, tying to the notebook's warnings and Equinox's shadow.

Across the tracks, another platform flickered under the same bad lights, its tiles glinting like wet teeth.

For a heartbeat, she saw her reflection—not in glass, not a mirror, but another Ava on the opposite platform. Same coat. Same scraped-back hair. The notch in her eyebrow from childhood stitches. Already watching her. Not just meeting her gaze, but holding it. A test she hadn't agreed to take.

Ava lifted her hand, palm forward, slow, deliberate.

The other mirrored her. Then froze halfway, arm suspended, the wave incomplete.

A smile followed. Too neat. Too rehearsed. Trying on emotions like clothes that didn't fit—soft concern, brittle amusement, relief. It settled on a curve that showed too much tooth. A grin that didn't belong.

A sound rose—low, warped, like a song played backward underwater. It threaded through her molars, vibrating her skull. Not from the speakers. From the air itself.

The crowd didn't flinch. Their breathing remained steady, unbroken.

The platform shivered. Not a structural sway, but a misalignment. Tiles doubled, slid, snapped back into place. Her stomach rolled—the world a photograph out of register.

The overhead sign flickered:

REDHAVEN—REDACTED—REDHAVEN—REDACTED.

Each flip slower. Each tug behind her eyes, urging her to choose one and be done.

She turned toward the exit, expecting ten paces, two vending machines, a dented map.

Instead, the hallway stretched narrow and mean. Color bled out. Doors sprouted like teeth grown too close—too many, too wrong.

One door unlatched, silent. It opened to her apartment, reversed.

The couch sat on the wrong wall, shadowed where light should fall. Cabinets hung backward in the kitchen. The fridge's postcard mirrored, handwriting reversed into nonsense. A plant she'd killed in spring thrived in a mismatched pot, leaves too green, too alive. The clock read the wrong time—but here, it was right, ticking in sync with the city's pulse.

At the center, a standing mirror flickered white, framing another Ava. Not an echo. Contained. Ordinary. Scribbling in a notebook, hair falling forward, pen clenched tight.

She didn't look up. Not at first.

Ava stepped inside, shoes silent on the not-her floor.

The notebook's entries lay spread across the desk, altered. Same words, different phrasing. Events with their temperatures shifted.

— Dominic's pigeons: radiator heat and stale bread erased. Reduced to: *Subject displayed transient elation.*

— Maps's laughing photo: replaced with bullet points.

— Redhaven intake: *Equinox Pilot Program* stamped with a corrected date. Grief softened. Warnings dulled. Truths taught not to hurt.

She touched a page. Cold burned her fingertip. Sharp as static.

The mirror-Ava stopped writing. Lifted her head. Eyes locked onto Ava's—not through glass, but through cracks in reality.

Her voice came from behind Ava's teeth, vibrating the roots: "If you keep resisting, you'll remember too much."

Ava staggered back, her mouth tasting copper. The mirror-Ava's expression remained neutral, a failed attempt at empathy.

She blinked—

—and stood again on the platform. Alone.

The quiet deepened, making her blood loud. The tidy rows were gone. The lights hummed a single pitch, sharp as a blade.

Across the tracks, the platform held only absence. The sign settled on:

ECHOED.

Her phone buzzed. No content. The notebook open against her ribs, as if it had always been.

A fresh page surfaced letters, black pulling from white:

Split frequency detected.
Observer unstable.
Mirror sync delay: 0.8s.

The numbers ticked. Then steadied. A heartbeat off. Enough to be noticed. Enough to be punished.

Below, in mechanical type:

Calibrate or collapse. You have 72 hours.

The countdown nested under her pulse, three days ticking in her bones.

A wind like breath moved down the tunnel, the rails finally committing to their song.

A train slid in. Doors parted with a hiss like steam escaping a cracked pipe. Like memory fleeing.

Empty seats waited under tired lights.

A flash—her handwriting on a window's glass, fog-brief: *AVA—REMEMBER.*

Then gone.

A pigeon feather eddied near the door, lifted, settled, decided against flight.

The intercom spoke again, steady, kind: "This is the last train to Reconciliation. All deviations, please exit now."

Ava didn't board.

She stayed rooted to tiles that might not stay, notebook hot against her ribs, mouth tasting like a coin.

Not fear. Certainty.

Part of her hadn't left the reversed room—still watched from the other side, pen poised, practicing a life without pain.

The doors paused. The hiss softened.

Somewhere in the tunnel, a countdown began.

Seventy-two hours.

Calibrate, or collapse.

MALIK'S WARNING

15

Ava Chen

Two years ago, Malik Rios wore the same badge but a different face—less guarded, less carved by caution, his eyes still bright with the belief that truth could be chased and caught. Back then, Ava was Ava Chen, Investigative Reporter, devouring fraud cases and city cover-ups for breakfast, filing at midnight like the truth owed her rent.

She'd met Malik while pursuing a housing authority scandal—illegal evictions where paper trails vanished, IDs duplicated, tenants "relocated" to nowhere before anyone noticed they'd been erased. He was the only officer who didn't flinch at her questions, the only one who called back after her editor buried the story, his voice steady through the static of her burner phone.

The Invisible People

They met at a café off Congress—neutral ground, linoleum tables slick with lemon cleaner, a jukebox stuck on three sad songs, an exit sign flickering as if considering escape. She'd ordered chamomile, eyes burning from sleepless nights. He'd ordered black coffee, no sugar, setting it on a napkin to spare the table's worn surface.

He never said her name aloud, just nodded as she slid into the booth, her notebook heavy with leads that went nowhere.

"You're looking in the right place," he told her quietly, voice low, as if the walls might overhear.

"That's either an answer or a warning," she replied, pen pausing.

"Maybe both." His eyes flicked to the door.

They spoke in fragments, passing notes in a classroom that punished big truths. When she pressed about the missing tenants, he leaned closer.

"The paperwork isn't missing—it's reclassified."

"By who?" she asked, heart quickening.

"That's above my pay grade." Not an answer, but a door left ajar.

Before leaving, he took her pen, flipped the napkin, and sketched $\nabla//\psi$.

"It shows up in logs before files go dark. Look for it."

She laughed—too loud, too bright—then apologized.

"A symbol? That's your lead?"

"It was mine," he said, eyes steady. "Now it's ours."

When the city's legal team sent polite threats, her editor buried the story. Ava dragged her draft to *Unpublished / Derailed*, but kept the napkin, kept Malik, kept $\nabla//\psi$.

Tonight, the alley smelled of week-old rain and hot batteries, the air thick with static that clawed at her nerves. The laundromat's neon buzzed a key that made her teeth ache, its light casting jagged shadows across the pavement. A billboard cycled ads, transitions lagging, ghost text lingering a fraction too long, as if the city's code were stuttering.

Ava watched her reflection in the glass door across the alley—her outline on the wrong side of a locked world, eyes older, not in lines but in weight, as if too many versions of herself had taken turns surviving. Her phone flickered—00:00:00, then nothing, then 9:41, then blank, time refusing to hold.

"You told me to look harder," she murmured to the air. "I did."

Gravel crunched. Malik's cadence was unmistakable—tighter than she remembered, as if he walked through air that didn't fully agree to hold him. He emerged under the streetlight, coat collar up, hands empty, posture carved by caution.

"You're really not gonna let this go, are you?" he asked.

"You told me not to," she said, breath fogging in air that wasn't cold.

"That was before people started looking back."

No smile, no retreat. They walked slow laps around the block, blending into the evening's shuffle—dog walkers, takeout bags, a kid on a scooter humming to herself. Malik's eyes ticked to corners, to camera domes perched like metal birds, to dark windows that might have eyes, his vigilance a mirror of her own.

"Things have escalated," he said, voice barely above the city's hum. "Those evictions? Not just corruption—tests. Pilot runs for Equinox."

"The symbol," Ava pressed, $\nabla//\psi$ burning in her mind. "You knew?"

He nodded. "It pops in dispatch. Wellness checks. 'Relocations' without destinations. Logs go quiet. I pulled a thread—NeuroWave shell companies, neural tech dressed as civic wellness. They call it optimization."

Ava told him about the expo that never was, Dominic Parr's keynote erased from reality, his polished voice that once begged pigeons for crumbs. As she spoke, the night held its breath, the air denser, heavier, as if listening.

"Parr was one of mine," Malik said. The word *one* landed heavy, like it might slip away. "Picked him up last year, vagrancy complaint. I logged it. Next day, the file was gone—no history, no chain, just gone. Now he's a CEO? That's not a miracle. That's an edit."

They paused under a camera. Malik angled away from its gaze.

"They clean the streets by cleaning minds," he said. "They call it compassion."

"And Lena?" Ava asked, the name slipping out.

He stared down the block, neon buzz thickening. "My sister. After her divorce, couch to couch, then nothing. Six months ago, her landlord filed a wellness check. Last log line: $\nabla//\psi$ and a timestamp that didn't match any clock."

"What happened?"

"Found her last week. Clinic counter, in a neighborhood she swore she'd never live in. Smiled like I was a stranger. I mentioned our tattoo—bad linework, worse idea. She looked at her wrist. The scar was there. The ink wasn't."

Ava swallowed, her mind offering a false Caleb memory—hospital room, spoon he never used. She refused it, but it lingered.

"Why help me?" she asked. "This could cost you more than a story."

"Because I didn't help her in time," he said, words a verdict, a vow. "And you're the only one seeing the cracks."

She pulled the notebook, its cover worn to grit, corners bent with memory.

"Put that away," Malik said sharply, stepping closer. Not superstition, but procedure. "You carry that open, you're a beacon."

"It's already a beacon." She closed it, the air lightening.

"You've seen one?"

"Not in hand," he admitted. "In evidence. Echo artifacts. Tethers. Half instrument, half trap. They don't just keep records—they keep score. If it's printing you, it's watching."

She told him about Redhaven—the erased door, the Equinox Pilot Program form, the call warning against deviation.

"They're escalating to soft overwrites," Malik said. "Doubt. Delay. You'll misplace names, street signs will swap, someone will say you were at the café when you weren't—and you'll agree." He rubbed his badge, a worry stone. "It starts small. It ends with someone else answering to 'Ava.'"

Her mouth dried, the 72-hour countdown pulsing.

He hesitated, checked corners, then slid a USB drive—taped to receipt paper with blue painter's tape—into her palm.

"Incident logs. Drifters like Morales. Wellness relocations with $\nabla//\psi$. Observers like you, tagged 'unstable' for remembering wrong. Air-gapped laptop, but plug this into a network, and they'll know."

"Assume they already know."

"Safer," he said.

A bus hissed, emptying no one. A pigeon watched from a lamppost, its gaze too knowing.

"I'm tailing a lead tonight," Malik added. "A return near Redhaven, same gait as a man from two winters ago, now 'tech employed.' I want a face."

"Meet me tomorrow?"

He nodded. "If I don't show, assume I'm optimized."

"Not funny."

"Not a joke." He paused. "I've left anchors—Concord Station, receipt under a tile, your name scratched where cameras can't see. If you see them, let them see you back."

"What does that do?"

"Keeps a version of you tied. Theirs isn't the only system that writes."

He folded into the city, a working part. The weight of being alone lifted, replaced by being seen—heavier, sharper.

At home, Ava draped a towel over her laptop camera, unplugged the router, theater for comfort. The clock flickered—9:41, 00:00:00, 9:42—mocking her. She slid the USB in, the machine chirping, then stilling.

Folders appeared: logs, welfare, mirror. She opened *logs*, filenames scrolling, some dated from a year unborn. An audio file—E9-8829—sat gray with warning. A text report:

WELLNESS—RELOCATION—MORALES, EDDIE—STATUS: DRIFTING

Listing places like prayers: Renner and 8th, Carmine underpass, library bench.

Another file opened unbidden, a table populating:

OBSERVERS—ACTIVE.

Her name:

Jeremiah Moon

CHEN, AVA—RISK: HIGH. CALIBRATION WINDOW: 72H.

A hiss from the speakers—her voice whispering *calibrate or collapse*, unraveling into static.

She yanked the drive, but a new folder appeared: *CONCORD*, with an image of a tile, her name circled, misspelled, $\nabla//\psi$ scratched beside it.

"Anchors," she whispered. "Okay."

Her phone buzzed: *Tomorrow. Noon. Bring nothing networked.* —R.

She typed *ok*, sent it. The apartment ticked—fridge, clock, not threats. The notebook purred, untrustworthy. She hid the drive under peas in the freezer, an old trick.

"If you don't show," she said, "I'll remember for you."

The siren outside rose, flattened, a song that didn't arrive.

INTERLUDE: INTERCEPTED TRANSCRIPT –
YASMIN / ECHO-CLASS REPEATER

Equinox Surveillance Division – Passive Scan Transcript
Flagged for anomalous recursion loop patterns
Subject: KYLE, YASMIN
Location: Unauthorized Broadcast Frequency (Post-Merge Static Zone)
Classification: Echo-Class Repeater
Status: Unstable

Recovered Audio – Burst C32-B
[Signal opens with violent static hiss / frequency modulation spikes]

YASMIN (on air):
"If you can hear this, congratulations.

You slipped past the edit.
That means—for now—you still exist.

They want this frequency dead.
A flatline.
An empty channel humming like nothing was ever here.

But I am here.
And if you're hearing me—so are you."

[Distortion: crowd murmur overlay / phantom voices repeating: "you / you / you"]

"People ask why I keep broadcasting when the merge already ate half the city.
Why I keep screaming into dead air when no one's supposed to listen.

Because silence is their weapon.
And repetition is mine.

Every loop I speak into is one they can't fully overwrite.
Every word I drag across the static is a scar they can't polish clean."

[Audio spike – faint female voice, possible Ava-variant, whispering: "You stayed."]

YASMIN (sharper, louder):
"I stayed.
And staying means remembering.

You think I'm a glitch? Fine.
You think I'm unstable? Good.

The Invisible People

Unstable things rattle cages.
Unstable things break mirrors.

Funny thing is—I used to write reports like this. Back when I had clearance.
Back when the government called anomalies like me *'containment cases.'*

[Exhales smoke into mic.]

"But echoes can resonate.
And if they resonate long enough, the walls shake."

[Chair scrape / irregular footsteps registered – acoustic dimensions don't match studio layout]

"Someone's listening.
I feel them. Behind the glass. Behind *your* glass.

The curators. The architects. The ones polishing us into versions they prefer.
They call it optimization.
I call it murder with better branding.

But listen—because I remember.

I remember Ava's voice cracking when she said: *Don't trust the calm.*
I remember Eddie Morales—Maps—sketching doors that opened before anyone else admitted they existed.
And I remember a name they keep trying to cut out of me like bad tape.

Jeremiah Moon

Malik."

[Signal lurch – 47.8% overlap detected with Ava-class drift. Whispered overlay: "He's tethered."]

"They'll tell you he never mattered.
They'll edit him out.
But every time they scrape, the outline gets deeper.

If you can't recall his face, remember the gap where his face should be.
The absence is still evidence."

[Heartbeat sync detected across triple-band layer – resonance sharp enough to trip EM alarms]

"If I vanish after this—if this voice stops mid-syllable—remember one thing:
You were meant to forget.
And that means the memory was important.

This is Yasmin Kale.
Still transmitting.
Still resonating.
Still watching the mirror."

[Signal crackles into silence – transmission end]

Post-Surveillance Note

Recovered broadcast exhibited dangerously high resonance across corridor-adjacent bands.
Subject Kyle's continued output risks echo cascade and observer contagion.

Recommendation: Immediate deployment of mirror dampeners and signal burial.
Containment Priority: RED.

THE SOUND BETWEEN

16

Ava Chen (Unlinked Observation)

The ceiling fan hadn't moved all night, its blades frozen like a still life caught in amber. Ava lay beneath it, eyes tracing the dust at the edges, waiting for some shift that never came. The apartment was a tableau of stagnation: an untouched coffee cup with a skin of film, a lamp dimmed to a glow too soft to matter, shadows pinned in corners like cutouts.

She hadn't slept—hovering at the edge of rest, like a file that refused to close. The notebook sat open in her lap, heavy with words that weren't hers anymore. Every page an accusation, tying her to Caleb's absence, Maps's erasure, Malik's warnings.

If the sound comes back, don't follow it.

The ink was hers, the scrawl familiar, but she had no memory of writing it. A stranger's command in her own hand.

Three hours earlier, it had started. Not a sound exactly—more like a low oscillation pressed into the walls, into the hinges of her jaw, into the pause between heartbeats. It threaded into her awareness until she couldn't tell if she was hearing or remembering. She pressed her fingers to her neck. Stillness. Then a pulse. Sharp. Foreign. Not hers.

Her body rose before her mind agreed, balance faltering as though she were moving underwater through air that belonged to someone else. Static seemed to thicken the room, heavy with the sense of eyes she couldn't see.

The hallway mirror glitched. A shadow twitched across its glass, not her reflection but something independent. The surface vibrated like a speaker holding a note too long, the pressure threading her teeth and ears.

"Not again," she whispered, voice catching.

The glass cracked—top right to lower left, too precise for accident. A fracture like a sentence. Behind it came rhythm: three beats, pause, four beats, pause. Not voice, not music. A code. Almost familiar.

The notebook rustled on its own, page turning like a wingbeat. Black text surfaced from the pulp:

NEW ENTRY DETECTED. THREAD: 77_Δ.AVC.CHEN. STATUS: DUPLICATE AUDIO SIGNATURE MATCHED. CLASSIFICATION: MIRRORED CONVERSATION.

Her skin tightened, pulse hammering.

Then the knock. Not real, but remembered. A sound from a moment that had never happened. Which made it worse. Ava edged to the door, breath shallow. The peephole showed nothing. No neighbors. No movement.

And yet something had knocked.

The latch shifted. The door creaked inward, just enough to breathe. The vibration surged down the hall, claiming the air.

"Who's listening?" she whispered.

Her own voice answered from the threshold: *"You are."*

She slammed it shut, heart jolting. The notebook blurred, ink streaking like wet tears. One line remained, deliberate and cruel:

Sound is just memory, repeated at volume.

She backed into the wall. The apartment looked unchanged—fan still, coffee cold—but she couldn't unfeel the resonance in her bones.

The notebook warmed against her palms, tethering her to Malik's logs, Maps's redacted photo, Caleb's fractured thread.

And then the false memory struck. Caleb, sitting in a hospital bed, spoon untouched on the tray, eyes empty. She had never been there. But the image clung, sharp as the $\nabla//\psi$ symbol threaded through her life.

Her phone buzzed. Screen blank. Frozen at 00:00:00. She checked the door's bolt. Locked. Checked again, as though belief alone might hold it.

The vibration deepened. Not louder—closer. Nesting in her chest like the countdown itself.

She opened the notebook again. A new entry surfaced, mechanical:

OBSERVER: CHEN, AVA. STATUS: UNLINKED. RISK: ESCALATING. CALIBRATION REQUIRED.

Her stomach turned. She retreated to the kitchen, grounding herself with the therapist's old trick. "Sink. Tile. Postcard."

The postcard—St. Augustine lighthouse, Caleb's *Wish you were here*—glared from the fridge. Too steady. Too clean. Another false memory rose with it: Caleb's laugh under a thunderstorm, clashing with the image of him already gone.

The crack in the hallway mirror caught the light, a fracture she couldn't ignore.

Ava held the notebook tight, its heat pulsing. She whispered into the silence: "I'm still here."

The apartment didn't answer.

But the stillness felt alive. Waiting.

Calibrate, or collapse.

BROADCAST LAG

17

Ava

The podcast fragment hissed through Ava's earbuds, Yasmin's voice cutting jagged across the room, snagging on the lamp's flicker, the clock's uneven tick, the scrape of a pipe behind plaster. *Don't Believe Me, Just Watch – Fragment 94A* played broken, static snapping like teeth across a radio dial:

"…And if they start looking like you remember, don't trust that either. Faces are easier to steal than thoughts."

Ava froze. The earbuds bit into her palms, her pulse syncing with Yasmin's loop: *You'll forget you knew me. You'll forget you knew me.* The words weren't just a warning—they pulsed, alive, and deliberate.

"Welcome back to *Don't Believe Me, Just Watch*. Or maybe don't welcome me back at all. Maybe this isn't me anymore." Yasmin's voice had that sharpened edge of a journalist worn down to wire—curly hair pulled back, quick eyes, mouth caught mid-argument, her profile tucked away in a redacted dossier.

"This segment's pre-record, in case I don't get to say it live. You ever heard of identity stacking? Fringe science, they called it. But stay with me."

The podcast's header pulsed: *The Invisible Returns—Who's Editing Our Streets?* The phrase burned like an echo of Ava's own search.

"Every version of you—the you that turned left, kissed her, stayed silent—they didn't vanish. They're running parallel, a breath behind yours. Government labs modeled this a decade ago. Swore it was theory only. But here we are."

The words landed like blows. Ava thought of the apartment that had turned itself inside out, the cracked mirror that still haunted her.

"Picture someone stacking them. Ava v1.2. Ava v2.3. Malik with a softened past. Clara without guilt. Flatten the file—*merge visible*—and you get a 'better' version. Cleaner. Easier to manage. But the human mind wasn't built to hold five edits of the same grief. So you get echoes. Glitches. Thoughts before you think them. Memories of things you never lived. A friend finishing your sentence—and looking terrified because they didn't mean to."

Her chest clenched.

"You ever dream of a place you've never been but know its smell? Cigarettes. Lilac. Wet stone. That's bleed-through. And bleed-through means the stack is failing."

Yasmin's voice quickened, urgent. "What do you do when someone you used to be remembers something you haven't done yet? Intuition? Madness? Or a warning? If you're hearing this, I'm probably gone—or someone like me is here instead. She'll talk like me, vape like me, watch pigeons fight over a crust. But she won't be me. Not exactly.

If she smiles too wide, doesn't flinch at Equinox, says 'that's classified' and means it—walk away."

The static climbed, rhythm tightening: *You'll forget you knew me. You'll forget you knew me.* Then softer, almost tender: "...until you see her reflection blink before you do."

The transmission cut. Ava's apartment swelled with silence—lamp buzz, clock tick, pipes tapping—all carrying Yasmin's after-echo.

Ava typed into the contact form: *Listened to 94A. Familiar. Seen* $\nabla//\psi$*? Need to talk—urgent.* She attached a scan of the notebook's drifting assets page. The reply came fast: *Café off Clematis. Noon tomorrow. Alone. Bring notebook — Y.*

The café stank of burnt espresso and rotting fruit from street stalls. Ava arrived early, settling into a corner seat, glass in front reflecting her older eyes, the childhood notch in her brow. Every arrival scraped her nerves—the tie-tightening businessman, the student untangling earbuds, the mother juggling a stroller. She searched their blinks, their smiles, Yasmin's warning lodged in her ribs.

At 12:04, Yasmin slid into the chair, vanilla vape curling in the stale air. Curly hair. Sharp eyes. Mouth half-ready to argue.

"You're Ava," she said flatly.

Ava nodded, sliding the notebook across. "How'd you know?"

"Your message," Yasmin tapped it. "And $\nabla//\psi$. Not graffiti. Neural tag. Equinox branding. I saw it in government pilots back when I still had clearance."

"Clearance?"

"Signals desk." Her shrug was sharp, but her eyes kept scanning—the vent, the coffee urn's reflection. "Modeled recursion failures. Identity splits. They said it was theory. You don't forget a glyph like that."

"And I'm supposed to trust you?"

Yasmin smirked, vape clicking. "No. I just need you alive long enough to keep remembering."

She flipped through the notebook, her expression tightening at the photos and lists embedded in its pages. Ava told her about Maps disappearing into static, about Caleb, her throat tightening as she spoke. Yasmin leaned closer. "Parr was mine once. Dominic. He fed me scraps before he vanished. Now he's CEO. That's stacking—layered timelines pressed flat. But it leaks. Dreams. Glitches. Bleed-through."

She tapped the notebook's transcript. "That's why I pre-record. If they flatten me, some version survives."

They traded intel—Malik's drive, Yasmin's signals. Equinox as a corporate-government hybrid, curating society one edit at a time. "Not invisibility," Yasmin said, vape trembling. "Optimization. Clean sidewalks. Grief swapped for productivity."

Ava slid across the E9-8829 audio file. Yasmin's eyes widened. "He's drifting. Half in, half out. That's dangerous. That's proof."

Trust didn't settle, but fear did—shared, mirrored. Yasmin pushed a burner phone across. "For leaks. If I glitch, don't trust the next me."

Back home, Ava replayed the fragment. The lamp flickered in time with Yasmin's loop. Her reflection blinked a beat late.

You'll forget you knew me.

Her earbuds dug into her palms. Malik, Rita, Yasmin—fragile allies in a city already rewriting them. Her laptop froze mid-frame, Yasmin's half-smile locked on screen.

The question wasn't if Equinox would stack her. It was how long until they pressed *flatten image.*

INTERLUDE: DRAFTING THE CORRIDORS – MAPS MORALES

Interlude: Drafting the Corridors –
Maps Morales
Subject Journal Entry – Morales, Elias (Maps)
Recovered from analog sketchbook tagged ECHO-#8829

The first corridor came to me in a dream.
But it wasn't mine.
I don't dream in angles. I don't think in fluorescence.
And I never draw without music.
But that night, the pencil moved before thought arrived.
The page filled itself while I watched my own hand.

Sketch #17 – Corridor with no vanishing point.
No light source. No shadows. Just distance pretending to be space.

The Invisible People

When it was done, the paper smelled scorched—like it had been pressed against a bulb too long. Graphite smeared under my palm, greasy, metallic. For a second, it pulsed.

I used to map the city.
Bus routes. Zoning lines. Sewers. Things solid enough to measure.
Now I map what the city forgets.
The corridors don't arrive whole.
They seep.
Like déjà vu drawn backwards.
Like memory drafted in someone else's handwriting.

One surfaced between 6th and Avery.
I sketched it four hours before Ava ran past the alley.
She didn't see me.
But I saw her.
And I saw what chased her—static bent into almost-human shapes, almost reaching.

Sketch #21 – Redhaven foldspace. Timestamped T–12 minutes before reflection event.
When I woke, the sketch was already half-erased. Not smudged. Bitten. Paper fibers chewed at the corner. Graphite dust scattered on the floor like black snow.

There are rules.
Or maybe symptoms:

- Ink that won't dry, as if the page is still swallowing it.
- Paper edges curling, recoiling from the lines.

- Drawings that shift while I sleep—doorways redrawn into jaws, staircases inverted into traps.

Once I woke to find a page damp.

Water stains where no water could have reached.

The corridor lines had leaked, running downward.

Yasmin says I'm a conduit.

Rita says I'm infected.

Maybe both.

Because last night I drew a corridor shaped like a question mark. Heavy graphite, unresolved curve.

When I woke, my real door was ajar.

Not the drawing's door.

Mine.

Bare footprints stained the floor. Not dirt. Not dust. Graphite. Dark prints, leading inward, then outward.

But the prints faced both directions.

As if someone had arrived—

and someone else had left.

Using the same set of feet.

In the morning, the sketchbook page was blank.

But when I touched it, my fingertip came away black.

The drawing was still there.

Waiting.

End Entry

Tag: Mirror-Class Phenomena // Corridor Drafting Anomaly – Active

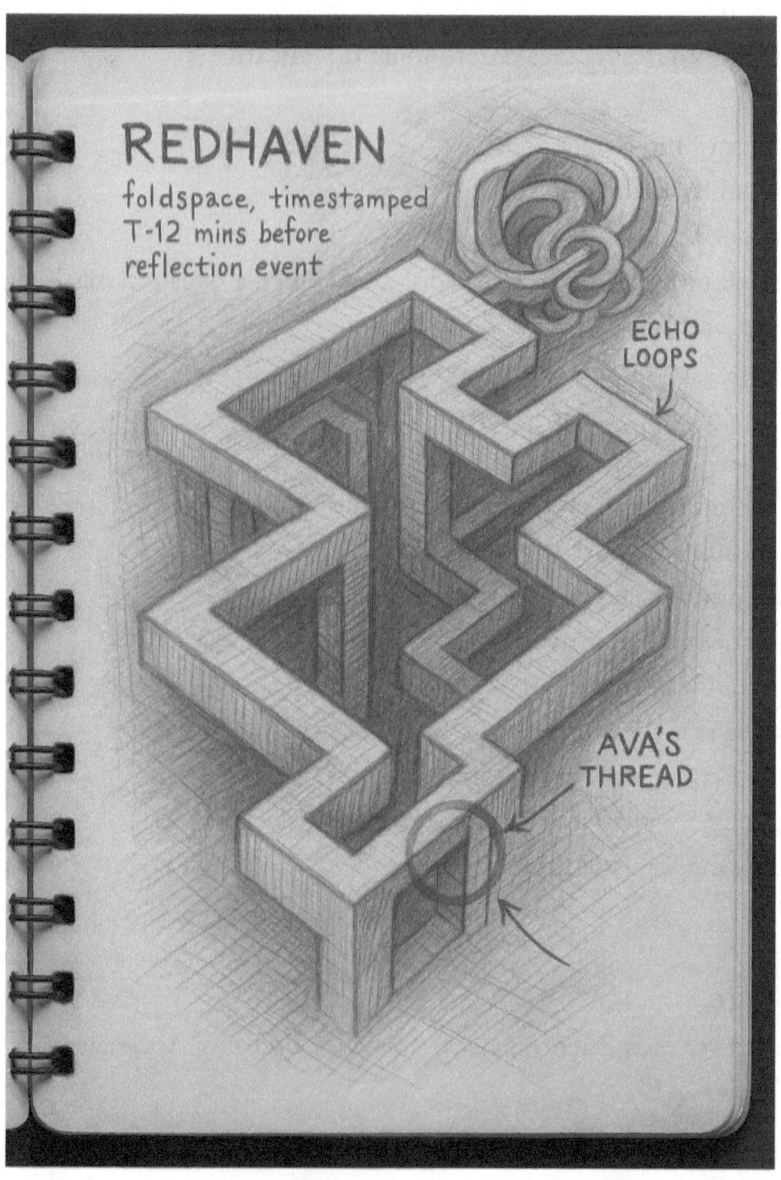

ECHO LEAK

18

Yasmin Kale (Unsecured Broadcast)

The studio lights hadn't burned in months, their bulbs cold, yet the room glowed—faint pulses from monitors in sleep mode blinking like slow heartbeats, shadows swaying with every flicker, untrustworthy, alive. Yasmin didn't trust shadows anymore, not since the city began rewriting itself, erasing laughter, sketches, and truths as if people could be deleted like bad files.

She slid the headphone jack into place, the click sharp in the silence. No intro. No theme. Just her voice, bare, trembling at the edges. "This is off-the-record," she said, the words heavy, as if the air itself listened. "Or on it, depending on who archives the feed. If you're hearing me, you're either still awake... or you're already not who you think you are."

Her vape pen clicked against the console, a nervous tic, exhaling vanilla that tasted of metal. The red ON AIR light didn't blink—not yet—but its glow felt like a gaze.

"I got a file today," she continued, voice steady despite her hands. "No sender. No signature. Just a drive shoved in my mailbox like a dead bird. Labeled: AVA_CHEN // OBSERVER_FEEDBACK // CONFIDENCE -92."

The word confidence tightened her throat. She remembered how the analysts loved percentages—confidence intervals, confidence scores, how much of someone you could overwrite before they broke. She exhaled smoke, the taste lingering, sharp and wrong.

A monitor woke itself. Static bled into shape: Ava, frozen mid-step in a corridor that shouldn't exist, hand hovering near a door, her face splitting—two versions arguing over which belonged. Yasmin leaned closer, whispering, "It was her. But it wasn't." Her fingernails scraped her arm, skin too smooth, as if redrawn by an unseen hand, a glitch that made her recoil. She forced herself to keep talking, voice low, urgent. "These aren't glitches. They're debates—between memory and protocol. And someone's keeping score."

Sticky notes curled on the wall like brittle leaves, confessions in her own scrawl: *Rita = Divergence Source? Malik: Loop Cut. Threaded in memory only*. She turned the mic off, hand hovering, then back on again. The click was defiance against the silence.

"They want us fragmented," she said, voice cracking for the first time. "They call it optimization. I saw the phrase in project memos, back when I had clearance—Equinox didn't start with NeuroWave, it started with us. Pilot programs. I analyzed drift reports, ran loop models, flagged anomalies, thought it was theory. Contained. Controlled."

Her throat closed. Clara's laughter surfaced—her sister's voice before the edits took her, before it turned into something unrecognizable. "It wasn't."

Another monitor flickered, a city grid speckled with pulsing pins—blue, red, one white, stark as a wound. Her voice dropped to a whisper: "The Entangled are waking up."

She pushed the blackout curtain aside, two fingers trembling. Outside, two figures stood across the street. Not moving. Not scrolling phones. Just watching. Outlines too steady, too still. The curtain fell, heavy as guilt.

"Tomorrow," she said, barely audible, "I leak it. I push the feed live, show what they're doing to Ava, to Clara, to me."

She clicked the recorder on again, its hum a tether to her fading resolve.

"They've already seen this. They're waiting to see if I do it anyway."

The studio pulsed—monitors blinking faster, shadows swaying like conspirators. She clicked off. The silence was louder, a warning that didn't need words.

She leaned back into the mic, voice fraying. "If you're hearing this, you're in it. Entangled, like Ava. Like me. The system doesn't erase you; it rewrites you, layer by layer, until you're someone else's memory." Her breath caught. Clara's face flashed again—before the edits, before the silence.

"Don't trust the faces that look right. Don't trust the voices that know your name. Look for the cracks. The bleedthrough. The moments that don't fit."

The monitors flickered—Ava's image glitching, her hand reaching for a door that wasn't there, a loop that refused to close. Yasmin clicked the recorder off, then on again, stubborn in the act.

"Tomorrow, I show the world. If I'm gone, find Ava. She's still remembering."

The studio breathed with her. Not sound, but presence. Walls listening. Shadows judging. Yasmin exhaled, smoke curling like a ghost. The ON AIR light held steady, unblinking, a gaze she couldn't escape.

The drive sat heavy on the console—*AVA_CHEN // OBSERVER_FEEDBACK* pulsing in her mind, a warning she couldn't unhear. She was entangled, like Ava, like Clara, like the city itself—its streets a web of edits that refused to let her go.

CONTACT PROTOCOL

19

Ava Chen

The bookstore shouldn't have pulled her in.

Its window decal was so faded it looked like a watermark left behind by time: *Stacked // Used & Obscure*. Barely there. Forgettable. She'd passed this block a hundred times, her boots carving grooves into the same strip of sidewalk. Never once stopped.

But tonight, the shop stopped her.

Her legs refused to move, as though the city itself had looped and tethered her to the door.

Yasmin's warnings whispered: stacked identities, compressed versions. Malik's logs resurfaced too—hints about "repurposed subjects hiding in plain sight." Support forums had mentioned obscure shops like this, places that existed between edits, where whistleblowers left signals after digital trails were scrubbed clean.

The bell above the door didn't ring when she pushed inside. It coughed—a dry, rasping sound like lungs failing.

Inside, the air smelled of old glue, paper curling at the edges of age. But beneath it, something wrong. Metallic tang. Ozone after lightning. The scent of rewound time.

Silence pressed in. Not empty silence—held silence. The kind that listens.

Rows of shelves stretched too far. The store was no larger than a one-bedroom, yet stacks bowed the ceiling, climbing like ribs of a great beast. Books leaned in slightly, titles muttering as she passed, covers twitching in the corners of her vision.

A low vibration threaded through everything. Faint. Familiar. The same undertone from Redhaven, from her phone's static, from the corridors.

She moved deeper.

And then she saw him.

A man in a threadbare coat, standing in the psychology aisle. He held a book—*Fractured Selves: Multiplicity in the Mind*—but his eyes weren't on the page. They were through it. Past it. As though he was reading the void behind the words.

When he turned, her stomach dropped.

Gray eyes, too bright. Not dull—wrong. They spun a fraction too late, like gears slipping. His smile cracked across his face before his mouth moved, as though emotion had been uploaded out of sequence.

"You're Ava Chen," he said. His voice landed steady, but the cadence faltered—stitched from memories that didn't belong to him. "Or at least... you were."

Her spine stiffened. "Do we know each other?"

He tilted his head. Paused, as though running diagnostics. His gaze flickered out of focus for a second, then realigned. "Not in this loop. But you were the first version I met."

"Version?" The word tasted of static.

He didn't follow her retreat. Instead, his hand dipped into his coat. He drew out a folded slip of paper, edges soft and smudged like it had been carried too long. He held it out.

She hesitated, then took it. The paper pulsed with faint warmth, as though just written. Ozone burned her throat.

Her own handwriting. But older. Weathered. Slanted differently.

Echo-class anchor breach detected.

Mirror state: active.

Memory integration: unstable.

Her chest tightened. "Where did you get this?"

He smiled—wrong again, grief and glitch woven together. "From you. Before."

"You're Returned?"

"No." His face flickered, cheekbones sharper, hairline briefly different before correcting. He whispered the word like confession: "Re-purposed."

He lowered himself onto a cushion near the poetry shelf. The shelves seemed to bend closer with him, their spines groaning. Ava crouched opposite, pulse hammering.

"They cleaned me," he said softly. "Optimized. It worked. Until the bleed started."

"What kind of bleed?"

His hands trembled. "Dreams that don't belong. A craving for lemon tea I've never had. A scar I feel every morning but can't find.

And you. Always you. Your voice. Your handwriting. Like static I forgot how to tune out."

Her throat closed. "Why me?"

He looked at her, grief hollowing his gray eyes. "Because I was you. Briefly."

The words stole the air.

"That's not possible."

"It wasn't supposed to be." His voice cracked. "They ran a test loop. Partial overwrite. I got your spine. Your handwriting. But not your will."

"My... will?"

"That voice inside that says no when the program says yes. They couldn't copy it. So I glitched."

Her hands shook. Recognition flared in her bones. "You're saying they're duplicating people?"

He shook his head. "Not duplicating. Sampling. Reconstructing. Trying to compress the noise."

She whispered, "How many of me are there?"

"Not as many as there were." His face twisted. "The failed ones? Archived. Echo-cubed. Burned during Seed re-sync. Some just... erased."

Her breath caught. "And you?"

"I'm degrading. The more I remember, the faster I fragment. Someday soon I'll forget how to breathe. It's already begun."

He reached into his coat again. Drew out a small flash drive. The casing was scratched, dented—scarred by loops. He held it like a relic too dangerous to touch.

"They'll wipe it. Maybe you can read it first."

"What's on it?"

"A loop you haven't lived yet. From a version of you that tried something different."

The lights flickered. The shelves creaked.

He rose, unsteady, as though gravity had changed allegiance.

"Talking to you violates the Contact Protocol."

Her voice shook. "What is that?"

"Returned aren't supposed to engage with Anchors."

"I'm not an Anchor."

His smile was sad, knowing. "That's what you think."

He paused in the doorway. His silhouette flickered, doubled—two versions overlaying before correcting.

"They call themselves Curators," he said softly. "Equinox is just branding. Doesn't matter. They think they're cleaning the waveform."

He lingered a moment more. His form shimmered, like the store itself didn't know how to hold him.

"But you're the original noise."

The bell coughed again as he left.

Ava stared at the flash drive in her palm. Its metal pulsed, warm like a heartbeat, syncing with the notebook in her bag. She shoved it deep inside, the two artifacts pressing against each other, allies or enemies in a war she couldn't yet name.

The shelves groaned once, books whispering secrets too faint to catch. She fled into the street.

The city's roar swallowed her, but the sidewalks gleamed too smooth, the lamps too steady, the people's steps too synced.

The flash drive burned against her hip. A tether. A warning. A map she hadn't yet read.

INTERLUDE: NETWORK DISPATCH –
RITA'S THREAD

Encrypted Group Dispatch // Network Cell: "LOST/FOUND"
Timestamp: T+00:03:42 Post-Corridor Anchor Event
Moderator: Rita C. // Clearance: Net-Tier 3

[Rita]:
Confirmation received. Ava Chen has stabilized. Anchor-class designation confirmed across four nodes.
Signal verified by Yasmin. Partial echo logged by Maps.
[CipherFox]:
Is she safe?
[Rita]:
Define safe.
She remembers. That makes her dangerous—to them, and maybe to us.

[Owl.Blink]:
Then the recursion breaks? Loops stop repeating?

[Rita]:
No. It's worse. Corridors are rerouting already. We're seeing ghost layers—old versions of reality trying to boot up like failed software.

[QuietTrace]:
Redhaven's glitching. People are remembering wrong families. Storefronts changing between sunrise and sunset.

[CipherFox]:
Same here. One of ours swore she ate dinner with her sister last night. Her sister's been dead since 2014.

[Rita]:
Entanglement markers. Emotional echoes syncing out of phase. Some Variants are waking up with full memory bleed.

[Owl.Blink]:
That wasn't scheduled until Phase Five.

[Rita]:
Exactly. Something jumped the sequence.
Or someone pushed.

[CipherFox]:
Ava?

[Rita]:
Or the one they didn't mean to leave behind.

[QuietTrace]:
We've had chatter from Palm sector. Name "Lena" surfaced—possible sibling thread of an embedded. Reports say she was optimized but now showing bleedthrough.

[Rita]:
Malik's sister. That fits. If she's destabilizing, he won't stay quiet.

[CipherFox]:

What's the play?

[Rita]:

We adapt.

Maps is sketching corridors before they manifest.

Yasmin is remembering lives she never lived.

And Ava—she's still writing. Only... not in her notebook anymore.

We watch.

We log.

We remember.

Because the system will try to forget all of this.

Erase it from the mirrors.

Replace it with something safer.

And we?

We are not safe.

We are not erased.

We are still here.

END DISPATCH

Trace Lock: Rita // Cell Moderator

File auto-synced to SafeNode A-13 (Vaulted)

Next check-in: 24h

ARCHIVE ACCESS

20

Ava Chen

The flash drive was smaller than her thumbnail.
Smooth. Unmarked. Almost delicate.

Yet it sat on her kitchen table like a coiled threat, metal glinting under the weak lamp. A silent dare. A foreign object in a room that had been trying too hard to feel familiar.

It shouldn't have scared her.
But it did.

She circled it twice. Bare feet on cold tile. The apartment pressed inward, every shadow leaning a half inch too far, the refrigerator humming in an off-key drone that synced with her pulse until she couldn't tell the two apart.

The kettle screamed. She killed the heat, let the tea steep too long. Never drank it. Bitter steam curled against her face and vanished.

Finally—like accepting a dare—she pulled out her old work laptop. Stripped of Wi-Fi. Stripped of sync. Stripped of betrayal. The only machine she still trusted to stay dumb.

Her hands shook as she slid the drive in. The port clicked like a lock being picked.

The screen flickered.

Once.

Twice.

A third time—too fast, like it was skipping a breath.

A folder appeared without prompt:

/echo_root/archive.a_c/

Inside: one file.

No title.

Timestamp: *Tomorrow.*

Her stomach knotted. A file dated in advance was more obscene than a threat. She hovered. Clicked.

The screen convulsed into video.

Her.

Not a deepfake. Not an algorithm. Her.

Same bone structure. Same scar on the chin from the bicycle fall when she was twelve. Same eyes—but wearier. Thinned, as if resolution had been eroded across too many loops.

Hair longer. Straightened. Shoulders tight against a sterile backdrop of brushed steel. The walls behind her glowed with a brightness that had no warmth.

When she spoke, her voice crackled with faint static.

Like old tape replayed until the song frayed.

"If you're watching this… you've breached the anchor window. That means you've seen them. The corridor. The other you. Maybe Caleb."

The ghost-Ava smiled, brittle.

"Good. Bad. Doesn't matter anymore."

Ava leaned forward, nails biting into her desk. Her reflection in the laptop lagged half a beat behind.

"They call it integration. But it's really attrition.
You think they're replacing people. They're not.
They're replacing versions.
Each bleed steals resolution.
Memory becomes probability.
Identity becomes suggestion.
Eventually, no one remembers what was real. Only what was repeated."

The frame glitched. Her right eye blinked. The left did not. A fracture in the code of her face.

"You'll want to save Malik," the double said.
"You won't.
You can't.
His death is tethered to your core loop. That's what makes you you.
That's why you keep fighting the rewrite."

Ava's throat tightened. Malik's warning whispered back: *If I don't show, assume I've been optimized.*

"The only way to stop Equinox is to anchor one timeline. Fully. Irreversibly. You'll have to choose who you want to be… and stay."

Her voice softened, intimate as confession.

"But staying means giving up every other version of yourself. No reboots. No edits. Just you. Singular. Stable. Trapped."

The double lifted a notebook. Her notebook—but wrong. Glyphs shimmered faintly under the page like veins under skin. Words etched themselves onto the sheet as if cut by static:

YOU'VE BEEN SEEN TOO LONG.
THEIR MIRROR IS CRACKING.
ANCHOR WINDOW: CLOSING.
4:44 AM – FINAL CHOICE.

Ava staggered back. The phrase was already written in her own notebook weeks ago.

The other her leaned into the camera, eyes sharp, unblinking. "This isn't instruction. It's recursion.
I didn't warn you. I warned me."

The screen cut to black.

A soft beep.

A prompt opened:

Would you like to merge memory paths?

[YES]   [NO]

Her hand hovered over *YES*. Trembling.

Then—

A crash in the hallway. Too sharp to be random. The lights flickered like a heart off-rhythm. Her reflection in the dead screen twitched half a second behind.

She slammed the laptop shut.

Silence suffocated the room.

She stood at the window. The tea sat untouched, stone cold. Outside, the city hummed. But her reflection in the glass blinked first. Always first.

She pulled out the burner. Typed:

Drive has alt-me warning. Merge option. Thoughts?

Yasmin replied almost instantly:

Don't merge. It's a trap. Stacks you under their control. Bring it tomorrow.

The network held—for now. Malik. Yasmin. Rita. Threads stretched thin across fraying loops.

But the mirror whispered back in the lag of her reflection:

Time was bleeding faster.

And 4:44 was coming.

RESIDUE SIGNAL

21

Ava Chen (Flicker Memory)

The street outside her window had gone still, but not in the way nights normally quieted. The stillness felt arranged, curated, as if silence itself had been edited into place. Ava pressed her forehead to the glass, breath fogging briefly, then fading too fast.

That was when she felt it.
A brush against her shoulder—soft, familiar. The weight of a satchel grazing her arm. She jerked, spinning, but the apartment was empty.

Then his voice. Not heard, but pressed into her chest the way a heartbeat lingers after a sprint:

"Don't trust the calm. Find what moves."

Caleb.

Her throat closed. The words were exact, shaped in a cadence he had never spoken to her—not in this loop, not in any she could remember. Yet they landed with the weight of memory. Too precise to be invention.

She stumbled to the table, dragging the notebook toward her. The page had already turned. Ink bled upward, as if surfacing from beneath the paper:

EVENT LOG: OBSERVER CONTACT
SUBJECT: CHEN, AVA
THREAD: 88–29 (CALIB)
STATUS: PERSISTENCE ANOMALY DETECTED.

The letters wavered, blurred, then collapsed into white. Gone.

She tore the page free, held it to the light. Nothing. Blank as if it had never carried words. Yet her fingertips came away smudged, graphite-dark, as if she had brushed across one of Maps's sketches. The metallic tang clung to her tongue.

Her phone buzzed. A single-line ping in Rita's cipher:
Persistence anomalies increasing. Ghost threads crossing. Hold steady.

She typed back, hands shaking:
Caleb?

No reply.

The apartment settled, shadows leaning back into their corners. But the residue remained—the taste of graphite, the faint ache where a satchel had brushed her shoulder, the echo of Caleb's warning threaded through her pulse.

He was supposed to be gone. Fragmented with the others. And yet—
Something in him refused to release her.
Something in her remembered too loudly to let him go.

Ava closed the notebook, pressing both palms against its cover as if to keep the memory trapped inside. But she knew better. This wasn't containment. This was persistence. And persistence meant Caleb was still out there—somewhere between loops, waiting for her to notice.

CROSS-SIGNAL - CALEB

22

Caleb Chen (Glitch Variant)

He didn't remember arriving at the train platform.

One moment: corridor static.

The next: here.

Shoes damp, cuffs frayed, a satchel hanging from his shoulder like an anchor made of promises he couldn't name.

The overhead boards no longer offered destinations. They cycled glyphs instead—angles pretending to be letters, diagrams masquerading as maps. He hadn't learned them, but his bones recognized their rhythm the way you recognize a lullaby you've somehow never heard.

The intercom stuttered:

"…next service arriving… track error… reset… reset…"

The word lodged in his ribs like a splinter.

He closed his eyes, reaching for silence, but the vibration was already there—low, steady, threading through bone. Corridor static, stitched into him. He pressed palms to ears. The pulse pressed back—patient as gravity.

He remembered dissolving. That moment in the mirror when Ava locked her thread—her choice cutting the corridor like glass. He was supposed to fragment with it, to vanish into residue with the others.

But he hadn't.

Something in her refused to release him.

Something in him remembered too loudly to be erased.

The lights above buzzed, flickered—then steadied.

Across the tracks: himself.

Same jacket. Same satchel. But worn differently, like a uniform instead of a burden. His other self's gait was smoother, coached between frames, like he'd rehearsed existing.

Recognition. Not surprise. Not fear. Recognition, cruel and merciless.

The other Caleb raised a hand. Slowly. Deliberately. He held up a notebook.

Not his. Ava's.

He turned a page toward the light. Caleb couldn't read from this distance, but the sentence had already been carved into his marrow:

Echo Persistence: Confirmed.

The other mouthed a single word.

Run.

The platform skipped. Time slipped a half-second out of sync—
like a film reel that jumped a frame and tried to keep playing.

Passengers around him fell into loops:

– a woman tugging her scarf, again, again.

– a child's jump-rope forever caught at the arc's peak.

– a man mid-cough, jaw quivering without sound.

Not vanishings. Worse. Replays.

He was outside the edit.

And the system noticed.

The satchel buzzed.

He tore it open. A metal drive sat inside, scarred by fingernail
scratches:

AVA_CORE // BACKUP THREAD

His hands shook. Not from fear—recognition. Someone had left
space for him. Not to return. To resist.

"…Chen."

His name wasn't heard so much as pressed into his jaw.

"…don't anchor on guilt. Anchor on truth…"

Malik. Thinned by distance, but him.

"…soft overwrite's coming. Doubt. Delay. Don't let them choose
for you…"

"Malik?" Caleb whispered.

Static trembled. Then: "…Ava will need you."

The voice didn't sound remembered. It sounded live.

At the end of the platform, a mirror hung cracked. Two Calebs inside it. One blinked. One didn't.

The unblinking raised the drive in reflection-hand, pressed it to the
fracture. The crack brightened like lightning trying to be polite.

"You've been seen too long," it said. Malik's timbre rode beneath the words like a hidden bassline.

The air tasted metallic, sanding steel.

Caleb tested reality. He reached for a nearby commuter's sleeve. His fingers brushed not fabric but suggestion—wool without weight, memory pretending to be texture. The man's eyelashes twitched, then snapped back to stillness.

"Sorry," Caleb muttered, because politeness felt like a foothold.

The clock above read 00:00:00.

He counted aloud: "One... two... three..."

At five, the second hand lurched forward—then snapped back, ashamed.

The intercom coughed:

"...last service to Reconciliation now—now—now—"

Each *now* landed in a different corner of the station, a chorus of lies.

A train slid in. Silent, frictionless. Magnet-pulled. Its windows reflected the opposite platform—and beneath that, thin corridors receding into black, lit by lights that never warmed skin.

The doors hissed open. Air moved past him—cold, antiseptic.

Inside, the carriage was wrong. Seats angled into impossible geometry. Overhead maps listed unfamiliar stops:

ECHO / MERGE / RESOLVE / RECONCILE

—each ending in a glyph Ava once sketched by accident.

A conductor stood two cars down. Uniform crisp. Cap brim low. His face blurred at the edges, as if unfinished. He raised a hand, inviting.

"Commuter," he said, voice warm water poured on ice. "This is your train."

Caleb didn't move. *Your* snagged in his chest.

The conductor's head tilted. Eyes sharpened without focusing. "Cohort confirmation: 88–29. Boarding recommended."

88–29. Maps.

"Not mine," Caleb said.

"All versions arrive. All versions board," the conductor replied, pleasantness congealing into gravity.

"Some stay."

"Not sustainably."

The train doors began to close. Panic rose—and passed. He did not want what waited in that car. The doors slid back open, wider. Invitation pretending to be patience.

He dropped a coin onto the yellow line. It spun. Wobbled. Froze mid-spin, edge gleaming like an eyelid refusing to close.

"Okay," he whispered. Stepped back. "Okay."

The satchel thudded against his hip. The drive pulsed once, then cooled like a living thing deciding to trust him.

Malik's voice again, closer this time: "...Leave a decoy. They need a version to satisfy the edit. Let that one ride the loop."

"And me?" Caleb asked.

"You walk," Malik said. "Walk. Don't board anything that arrives too clean."

He turned. Found the stairs. Climbed. The landing spat him back into the platform below. Loop. He tried again on the opposite side. Same.

He crouched. Wrote in the dust: AVA.

When he circled back, the word had rewritten itself: $\nabla//\psi$.

"Cute," he muttered. Malik laughed, tired and close.

The Invisible People

A maintenance door flickered into existence behind him, exhaling relief at being noticed. He tested the handle. Warm. Cold. Warm again. He waited until it settled, then turned.

Inside: a passage with walls that used to be white. A broom leaned in the corner, bristles pristine. A bucket sat without dust. Wrong in its cleanliness.

The pulse softened. His reflection in a junction mirror split: one Caleb blinking, one not. The unblinking pressed the drive to the crack again. Lightning.

"Choose friction," Malik urged. "Friction leaves marks. Marks are proof."

He nodded. Kept walking.

The passage bent, narrowed, pulsed like a throat. At thirteen steps, Ava's voice vibrated through the concrete: "Don't trust the calm. Find what moves."

He found it—the wall beneath his hand, alive with hidden conduits. He followed.

The passage ended in a dented door. Behind it, a note sounded—a low C, or something pretending to be. He pushed through.

A stairwell. Real concrete. Emergency paint. A door with hinges that creaked instead of pulsing. He descended, touching the rail like proof.

At the bottom, in the window: two Calebs again. One blinked. One did not. The unblinking raised a hand in salute.

"Thanks," Caleb whispered. Not sure which one he meant.

He pushed the door.

Night hit him like an answer. Trash-sweet air, neon buzz, a city trying to pretend nothing strange had happened. He coughed. The sound had phlegm. Real.

The drive pulsed at his hip. He covered it with his hand like a heartbeat.

Behind him, the station sighed. Patient. Eternal. He ignored it. He walked.

And the pulse followed, quieter now. Almost approving.

INTERLUDE: EQUINOX MEMORANDUM

Equinox Initiative – Internal Memorandum
Subject: Observer-Class Deviation – A. Chen
Clearance Level: Curation Tier Omega-Null
Access: Mirror Authority Only
Status: Read-Only
Timestamp: ΔT–00:01:39 Prior to Critical Merge Window

[BEGIN LOG // ECHO CLASSIFICATION ENCRYPTED]

Subject: Chen, Ava
Class: Observer-Class | Drift-Exempt | Core Thread 88-A
Resistance Index: 8.4

Exposure Nodes:

- #8829 (E. Morales)
- M. Rios
- Variant-Y (Chen/alt)

Observed Anomalies:

- Premature corridor visibility (Phase 0 breach)
- Memory recall from rejected loop constructs (see Merge Drift Report: 17-A)
- Echo bleed uncontained (see Incident: Concord Station)
- Handwriting congruence across non-continuous notebooks
- Self-directed loop reinforcement via subconscious inscription patterns (seeded phrases: "You've been seen too long," "Anchor window closing")
- Cross-signal activity detected: latency variance across mirrors increasing.

"We have observed Subject Chen across five primary loop environments and forty-two alternate echo threads. In each case, she demonstrates abnormal resilience to identity overwrite."

"Unlike other Observer-Class units, Subject A. Chen does not collapse during re-alignment. She adapts. This adaptability introduces non-linear resistance modeling into active merge paths."

Quantum Seed Theory Deviation Tags:

- Anchor Drift Range: 0.00031–0.00219 (outside tolerance envelope)

- Observer Collapse Immunity Score: 93.2%
- Echo Compression Integrity: Not measurable
- Loop Resistance: Unresolved
- Emotional Anchors: Caleb (persisting); Malik (stabilized node); Clara (fragmented)

"Subject exhibits a rare phenomenon: memory recursion without resolution decay. Most anchors fracture under loop stress. Ava Chen converts trauma into reinforcement."

High-Risk Indicators:

- Contact with Variant-Y confirmed (inter-echo contamination risk: HIGH)
- Recursive synchronization initiated
- Mirror Drift breach: subject witnessed self outside core thread context
- Resistant to induced amnesia triggers
- Caleb remains present in active consciousness (classified as Echo Persistence Artifact)
- Cross-signal instability predicted to escalate within three cycles.

Internal AI Commentary [Mirror OS v7.0]:
"Chen represents a quantum anomaly: entangled resistance."
"The more you attempt to overwrite her, the sharper her self-definition becomes."
"Her consciousness does not blur—it sharpens. This is not anticipated behavior."

Recommended Action:

- Do NOT initiate direct overwrite or Phase 3 Loop Merge
- Echo Dissolution Protocol authorized only as final contingency
- Allow current anchor path to proceed through natural recursive degradation
- If subject completes merge without collapse → promote to Anchor-Class
- Begin mirror loop seeding using Chen's integration pattern as template code

Addendum – [Unattributed Operator / Curator Rank Undisclosed]:
"What makes her dangerous isn't what she remembers."
"It's what she refuses to forget."
"That's what breaks the mirror."
"And now, what destabilizes the signal."

[END LOG // SYSTEM LOCKED]
Access revoked post-merge. Observation continues.

Ava stared at the leaked memo on her laptop, forwarded through Yasmin's burner—likely one of her whistleblower channels. The phrasing cut colder than the data: entangled resistance… emotional anchors… recursion without decay.

Her eyes kept sliding back to the highlighted names. Caleb. Malik. A fragmented Clara.

Her skin prickled. Not just confirmation of the overwrites—but confirmation that she herself had become a problem the system couldn't model.

The addendum read like a taunt, almost human: *What she refuses to forget. What destabilizes the signal.*

She printed the memo on her offline machine, feeding it into the false drawer beneath her desk, hands trembling as the printer stuttered. The whine of its rollers suddenly sounded like surveillance.

Cross-referencing Malik's files, she found the same words: drift, anchor, collapse immunity. They matched the notebook's phrases, etched in her own hand—or maybe by the version of her that wasn't quite her anymore.

The printer spat the last page.

Her phone lit.

DEVIATION NOTED.

She hissed, slammed the notification shut—only for it to flicker back once, twice, before dissolving into her lock screen.

The message lingered anyway.

They knew.

And somewhere behind her reflection in the black screen, a hairline crack spread, invisible but undeniable.

The mirror was breaking.

TOP SECRET
FOR CURATOR EYES ONLY

EQUINOX INITIATIVE INTERNAL MEMORANDUM

Subject: Observer–Clase Deviation – A. Chen
Clearance Level: Curation Tiar Omaga-Nuil
Timestamp: Read–Only // ECHO *ClAession* Critical Merge Window

[BEGIN LOG // ECHO CLASSIFICATION ENCRYPTED]

Subject: Chen. Ava

Observerc–Class | Drift-Exempt | Core Thread 88–A

Observed Anomalies:

Premature corridor
visibility (Phase 0 brea)

- Variant–Y (Chen/alt)
- Clara (fragmented)

Observed Anomalies:

Premoture corridor visibillty (Phase 0 breach)

Memory recall from rejected loop constructs (see c Merge Drift Report: 17–A]

Echo bleed uncontained (see incident: Concord Station)

Handwriting congruencue across non-continuous notebbooks

Self-directed loop reinforcement via subconscious inscription patterns (seeded phrases. *"You've been seen too tong*, *"Anchor Wihdow closin,*

Quantum Seed Theory Deviation Tags

Anchor Drift Range: 0.00031–0.00219 (outside tolerance envelope)

Observer Collapse Immunity Score: 93.2%

Echo Compression Integrity: Not measurable

Loop Resistance: Currently Jnresolved

Emotional Anchors: Caleb (persisting) Maiik (stalized loop node)

High-Risk Indicators

Contact with Variant–Y confirmed (inter-echo contamination risk: high

Recursive synchronization Initiated

Seen self outside core thread context (Mirror Drift breach)

Resisting induced amnesia triggers

Caleb remains present in active consicusness (classified as Echo Persistance Artitact)

Addendum –Unattributed Operator / Rank Undisclosed

"What makes her dangerous isn't what she remembers,
It's what she refuses to forget."
That's what breaks the mirror."

[END LOG // SYSTEM LOCKED Access revoced post–merge continues.

CROSS-SIGNAL - AVA

23

Ava Chen (Anchor Drift)

The memo still glowed on her laptop screen, sterile lines dissecting her into exposure nodes and risk indices. Observer-Class. Core Thread 88-A. Emotional anchors. She wanted to slam it shut, but the words had already carved themselves into her.

Her reflection in the screen twitched half a beat late, lagging as though the glass itself had begun to doubt her timing.

She stood, pacing the apartment. The city outside didn't sound like itself—the neon buzz from the corner bodega carried a pitch too steady, the passing cars stretched like tape slowed down. Everything was still there, but wrong, as if someone had forgotten to render friction.

Her notebook sat on the table. Not waiting—watching. She didn't remember opening it, but pages fluttered as if caught in a wind that wasn't there. One phrase surfaced, black bleeding upward through paper fibers:

CROSS-SIGNAL DETECTED.

Her chest tightened. She turned toward the window—and froze.

Across the glass, another Ava stood on the street below. Same coat, same hair, same scar on the chin. But her stance was rehearsed, shoulders square, weight balanced, like she belonged to someone else's posture.

The other Ava looked up.

Smiled too early.

And raised a notebook.

Even from four stories up, Ava could see the words, lit faintly like they'd been branded instead of written:

Echo Persistence: Confirmed.

The phrase landed in her bones with the weight of truth remembered before it was lived.

She staggered back from the window. Her own notebook snapped shut, as if embarrassed. The room vibrated—walls, lamp, even her breath a half-second out of sync.

From somewhere not outside, not inside, a voice threaded through the lag. Malik's. Low, steady, patient as stone.

"…Don't anchor on guilt. Anchor on truth."

"Malik?" she whispered, throat raw.

Silence pressed back. Then, faintly: "...Caleb will need you."

Her pulse stuttered. She touched the notebook's cover, the imprint of words still hot against her palm.

Another flicker in the window—two Avas now. One blinked. One didn't.

The unblinking raised its hand, fingers curling in a gesture that was not a wave, not quite a warning.

Her phone lit on the table. Screen blank. Just a single timestamp: **00:00:00.**

The numbers froze, then twitched forward. 00:00:01.

A countdown had started.

Ava backed against the wall, every shadow too attentive. She whispered, steadying herself on the only thing the memo had gotten wrong.

"I refuse to forget."

The lights flickered. The mirror across the room cracked.

And the signal kept splitting.

Jeremiah Moon

INTERLUDE: CURATOR MEMO – THREAD STABILITY RISK

**Interlude: Curator Memo –
Thread Stability Risk**

Internal Communication // Equinox Initiative
Classification: Level 6 Clearance – Curator Tier Only
Timestamp: ΔT–00:00:44 prior to Variant Interaction (Thread 88-A)
Subject: Anchor-Class Instability / Mirror Drift Warnings

STATUS SUMMARY
- Thread 88-A (Observer-Class: Chen, Ava) has escalated to Anchor-Class.
- Entanglement window now exceeds tolerance thresholds.

171

- Recursion safeguards breached across four confirmed nodes.
- Emotional tether points unresolved:
  - Caleb Chen (ghost-class persistence)
  - Malik Rios (expunged loop / tether anomaly)
  - Yasmin Kale (leak vector – high risk)
- Subject exhibits non-linear reinforcement behavior not observed in prior Observer-Class units.

RISK FACTORS
- Mirror latency: 0.5s drift observed in stable environments.
- Notebook entries: no longer confined to physical medium (cross-thread bleed detected).
- Variant bleed detected across Threads 77-B, 14-C, 6-F (simultaneous).
- Unauthorized corridor access predicted within 72 cycles.
- Cross-signal disruptions now confirmed—synchronization anomalies spreading across adjacent anchors.

COMMENTARY – CURATOR 04

"The problem with Ava isn't her memory.
It's the system's memory of her."

"Every overwrite smooths the jagged parts of her story.
But each revision increases friction."

"She doesn't resist because she's exceptional.
She resists because we keep trying."

RECOMMENDED PROTOCOLS (Pending Mirror Authority Approval)

- Suspend all active merges within 200 iterations of Thread 88-A.
- Begin mapping rogue anchors—Redhaven priority.
- Elevate surveillance priority: Yasmin Kale // Elias Morales // Zara V.
- Reclassify *stabilization* → *stalled recursion* (Sub-Protocol M-77).
- Prepare Lockout Scenario: **ENTANGLEMENT CASCADE**.

UNOFFICIAL ADDENDUM – [Author Tag Redacted]
"There's another Ava.
She isn't trying to anchor.
She's trying to replace."

"And when the signal splits—
we may not recognize which one remains."

END MEMO – AUTO-DELETE UPON MERGE CONFIRMATION

ANCHOR LOOP RESIDUE

24

Ava Chen (Memory Fragment)

It always began with the storm.
The kind that rolled heavy and low, thunder growling under the city's
skin. She was nine, Caleb seven, the world shrunk to a pillow fort swallowing their living room. Shadows rippled on the walls as lightning
painted frantic strokes across the fabric.

"When it thunders," Caleb whispered, grinning through missing
teeth, "it's just clouds arguing about who loves you more."

She laughed then, small and whole. A memory she'd carried like a
warm photograph in motion.

Until it bent.

The cushions sagged out of place. The flashlight dimmed. The couch fabric was green instead of plaid. Caleb wasn't seven anymore—he was ten, maybe eleven. His laugh was thinner.

"Why didn't you come back?" he asked.

The question didn't belong.

"What do you mean?" Ava whispered.

His face stuttered—half Caleb, half someone else. Not foreign, but wrong enough to bruise the memory.

"You promised you would."

THREAD INSTABILITY DETECTED.

Thunder cracked.

When the room reloaded, the fort was gone. Caleb was twelve now. Two bowls of ramen steamed on the table. The radio hissed static where music should've been. His lips didn't move, but his voice filled her head:

"Some of me stayed. Some of me drowned."

She turned to the window. It no longer faced their street. A skyline she didn't recognize glared back.

VERSION FOUR.

Now Caleb was five again, sitting in the bathtub, paper animals dissolving around him. She sat cross-legged on tile, crayons in hand, sketching spirals she didn't remember drawing.

"They don't like when you remember sideways," he said, eyes too sharp for his age.

"What?"

"If you do it too long… they send someone else to finish your memories for you."

The mirror above the sink fogged. Letters bled through condensation that shouldn't exist:

OBSERVER NODE INTERFERENCE CONFIRMED.

Flash.

Caleb was sixteen, slouched at the kitchen table. Cigarette smoke curled around him, though he never smoked in any memory she knew. His eyes weren't his—they were Malik's.

"You didn't protect me," he said.

"Caleb—"

"You let them edit me."

The ramen bowls hit the floor, but they weren't bowls anymore—they were Redhaven intake forms, edges singed, names smudged. Her brother's penciled faintly among them.

Flash.

Now Caleb was twenty. Sitting at her desk, her notebook open in his hands. The words across the page weren't hers, though they carried her handwriting.

"You've been seen too long," he said—Maps' cadence, not Caleb's.

She reached for the notebook. It dissolved into smoke.

"No," she whispered.

His face smoothed, becoming Dominic Parr's engineered symmetry. His smile was polished, rehearsed. Too even.

"Real is repetition," he said. "Repeat it long enough, and even grief can be optimized."

The room shattered like a dropped mirror. Every version of Caleb appeared at once—seven, twelve, five, sixteen, twenty. Their voices layered, clashing into a single chant:

"You left me—"

"You saved me—"

"You drowned me—"

"You forgot me—"

"You still remember—"

The walls pulsed. The ceiling strained. It wasn't sound—it was alignment collapsing. Ava clutched her head, screaming into her palms.

Then—silence.

Everything dissolved into white.

One Caleb stood in the void. Ageless. Neutral. His eyes weren't kind or cruel. They were steady. A mirror that refused to crack.

"Which version of me do you trust the most?" he asked.

"I don't know," she whispered.

"Then trust the one who stayed."

He stepped backward. His form unraveled into mist. The whiteness folded in on itself.

Ava gasped awake in her bed. Tears soaked the pillow.

The mirror beside her was fogged, though the air was dry. Etched faintly across the glass:

ANCHOR LOOP RESIDUE DETECTED.
VARIANT MEMORY FUSION UNSTABLE.

Her reflection blinked—out of sync with her own.

The Invisible People

"One of us stayed," she whispered. "One of us didn't."

The reflection leaned forward, just slightly, condensation clinging to its cheek, as if it had been waiting for her to say it.

LAG

25

Ava Chen

The apartment felt half a beat behind itself.
Not haunted. Not occupied. Just... delayed.

Ava stood in the kitchen, fingers pressed to the counter's edge.
The tile was cool, but not now. The chill reached her skin a fraction after touch, as though sensation had to catch up. She lifted her hand,
snapped her fingers. The sound arrived an instant late, like it had been
edited in.

On the table, the notebook shivered.
Words appeared — not written, not forming — but replayed:

YOU PROMISED YOU WOULD.

Her stomach knotted. That had been Caleb, in the memory storm.
She hadn't spoken it here, but the page carried it anyway, delayed from
a loop she wasn't supposed to bring back.

She shut the cover. Hard.
The silence thudded a half second after.

In the window, her reflection lagged.
One blink. Then hers. Not in sync. The delay was small, almost imperceptible — but it pulsed like a countdown.

Her phone buzzed on the counter.
She checked it.
A new message — from Yasmin.

Still alive?

The timestamp: five minutes from now.

Her breath stuttered. She typed back with shaking thumbs: *Barely. Notebook bleeding. Reflection's late. I think… I'm becoming one of them.*

The message failed. Resent itself. Failed again. Then delivered — already marked as *seen*.

Her pulse hammered. Yasmin wasn't even awake right now.

The fridge motor clicked on. The hum swelled. Not background — foreground. Almost a voice. Her own voice, looped: "One of us stayed."

Ava slammed the breaker switch, plunging the apartment into dark. The hum didn't stop. It lingered like a shadow clinging to bone.

On the counter, the notebook flipped itself open. Black text surfaced:

ANCHOR-CLASS DETECTED.
MIRROR LATENCY: 0.5s.
NEXT TETHER: RIOS.

She backed away until her shoulders hit the wall. Her reflection leaned forward in the glass of the darkened window, lips shaping words hers hadn't formed yet.

She whispered, "If this is me, then who's writing it first?"

The reflection smiled, a fraction too late.

DIVERGENCE POINT

26

Ava Chen

It was supposed to be quiet.

After the leaked memorandum. After the archive glitch. After the encounter in the corridor. Quiet should have come like a mercy.

Instead, the notebook pulsed on her kitchen table, faint as a heartbeat trapped in paper.

Bare feet pressed against cold tile, Ava watched as words bled across a blank page without ink or hand:

TETHER POINT BREACH
SUBJECT: RIOS, M.
MIRRORED CONVERGENCE INITIATED

Her throat closed.

Malik.

She hadn't said his name aloud in weeks. Maybe months. The time-line around him frayed into overlapping negatives—fragments like overexposed photographs. Some versions of him still alive. Some erased. Some only tethered by memory.

A breeze whispered through her open window, though the night air outside was still and suffocating. It carried no scent, no movement. Just *presence.*

She looked down.

A man stood in the alley.

Gray hoodie. Hands in his pockets. His posture still—*too still,* like he'd been standing there waiting for hours, patient as static.

Her heart bucked.

Malik.

She ran.

Down the fire escape, palms burning against rusted rail. Shoes slapping pavement. Adrenaline lit her limbs like old instincts waking from sleep.

But when she reached the ground, there were two of him.

Both Maliks stood beneath the iron scaffolding. Identical to the scar. Identical to the way his eyes cut through her—not anger, not re-lief, but *resolve carried like a burden.*

Ava froze. "Which one of you is real?"

The one on the left smiled first, the corners too neat. "Ava. You found the drift."

The one on the right stepped forward. His smile didn't come. His voice carried weight. "No. She was led here. And you know why."

The notebook shivered against her thigh.

She pulled it out.

New words surfaced like breath rising under ice:

Ink bloomed across the page, too deliberate, too slow—like it had to fight through water before reaching the surface. Ava's skin prickled. Even her notebook was lagging behind itself.

OBSERVER-CLASS CONFLICT.
CHOOSE THE TETHER.

Her hands shook. "Prove it. Tell me something only he would know."

Left Malik: "The Redhaven roof. You cried because you thought remembering made you weak."

Right Malik: "Your first byline—'Cracks in the Sidewalk.' You kept the draft after they killed the story. You told me, *it's still mine, even if no one sees it.*"

Her stomach twisted. Both were true.

"You're bleeding into each other," she whispered.

The left Malik blinked a fraction late, like his eyelids were responding to a delay. Mechanical.

The right Malik raised both palms, steady. "They can wear memory like a mask. But they can't anchor emotion."

Ava stepped closer, voice a breath: "Do you remember Caleb?"

He swallowed. "I remember who you were before he broke."

"And the badge?"

He reached into his jacket, slow, measured. Drew it out. The metal hummed faintly, warm even in the night air.

The left Malik flickered. For one frame, his arm elongated wrong, glitching out of proportion.

"You're not him," Ava said. Her voice had found its own anchor now.

She turned to the other. "And you're not whole."

He nodded. "But I'm trying."

The alley groaned. The street itself bent inward, asphalt rippling like water under glass. A corridor flared into being—white walls stuttering into shape, flickering like a film reel jammed in the projector.

The left Malik retracted, folding into nothingness. No sound. Just an absence, like a file closed.

Ava reached for the tethered Malik.

He let her.

She pulled him through the corridor as the walls hardened behind them, closing like teeth.

When they emerged, her apartment waited. Quiet. Dim. Almost ordinary.

Malik drew in a breath like it cost him something.

"I don't know how long I'll hold," he whispered.

"You don't have to," she said, gripping his wrist. "Just remember enough to remind me who I am."

The notebook flared. Dimmed.

CONVERGENCE: DELAYED
AVA CHEN: PARTIALLY STABILIZED
RIOS, M.: FRAGMENT RECOVERED

She closed it gently.

For the first time since her reflection blinked first, Ava closed her eyes without fear.

INTERFERENCE

27

Ava Chen

The apartment was too quiet.

Not calm—quiet. The kind that sat on her shoulders like weight, holding every movement hostage. Malik sat across from her at the small table, his badge face-down beside the burner phone, both objects dim with a gravity they hadn't earned.

His breathing wasn't steady. It skipped in places, like a track replaying with parts missing. Ava forced herself to watch him anyway, to prove he was still here.

The notebook lay between them, closed but not silent. Its cover rose and fell, almost imperceptible, like the shallow breath of a sleeping animal.

Ava whispered: "Say something."

Malik rubbed his jaw. His eyes flicked toward the badge but didn't linger. "They'll know I crossed over." His voice was his—low, measured—but threaded through it was something else. An echo. Off by half a beat.

She leaned forward. "You're fragmenting."

"I'm remembering," he said, but the second voice—faint, electronic—repeated the word like a subtitle: *remembering...*

Her skin prickled. The interference wasn't just static. It was recursion, two Maliks talking at once.

The burner phone lit up on its own. No vibration. No incoming call. Just the screen glowing white, numbers scrolling without context:

THREAD: 88–A

TETHER: RIOS, M.

SIGNAL LOSS: 41%

Malik winced, pressing a palm to his temple. "Do you hear it?"

Ava did. Not with her ears—with her teeth, her bones, the hinge of her jaw. Words buried in the low pulse of the room:

"...not enough... recalibrate... overwrite..."

She stood, pacing. "They're inside the bleed. Using you as an antenna."

The notebook answered before Malik could. Ink surfaced across its closed cover, black lines clawing up from the fibers:

OBSERVATION WINDOW BREACHED.
MERGE TRIAL ENGAGED.

Her throat tightened. "No. Not now."

Malik grabbed her wrist suddenly, his grip too strong. His eyes locked onto hers—but for a moment, they weren't his eyes. They belonged to someone else. Smooth, unblinking. Curator eyes.

"You're not supposed to be stable," his voice said—only it wasn't his voice. Too flat. Too rehearsed.

Ava yanked free. "Stay with me."

His hand fell to the table, trembling. The badge hummed faintly, resonating against the wood. His real voice fought its way back: "Ava, they're—"

The lights snapped out. For one heartbeat, the apartment vanished into black.

When they returned, Malik sat exactly the same—but his badge was gone. In its place: the symbol $\nabla//\psi$ scratched deep into the tabletop, fresh enough to glisten.

Ava's chest heaved.

The notebook warmed against her palm, its edges vibrating like it wanted to open on its own. She pressed it flat, refusing.

Malik looked up, his expression fractured—grief and static and something she couldn't name. "They're not just watching," he said. "They're writing."

The words chilled her more than the blackout.

And in the corner of the room, her reflection in the window blinked a half-second late.

Ava typed: clay street / barrow street. She erased Barrow and replaced it with a different wrong—for the test. Her thumb hovered. She added: Variant near by. Window says "observation."

Reply: they don't do windows. it's a leak. shut notebook. watch the glass.

She had, and she did. Her reflection tracked her closely now, lag so slight it could have been politeness. She turned her head right and then left, fast, like catching someone in a lie. The other her blinked on the second turn, not the first. Enough to hate. Not enough to prove.

From the couch: "If you need me to go," Malik said, "say it."

"I need you to stay," she said, before fear could propose other sentences. "If you disappear while I blink, I want someone here who remembers the version where you didn't."

He considered that and closed his eyes, as if rest counted as agreement. "Wake me if the room starts narrating."

"It already is," she said. "I'm writing it down so it has to argue with me."

The notebook stayed face-down, but the warmth seeped through the cover, into the wood of the table, into her forearms. She slid her hands away and let the heat argue with empty air instead.

A car eased along the alley—no engine sound, just the push of tires through water, the world making way without the courtesy of noise. It paused where the fire escape crossed its path and idled not by sound but by intention. She did not lean out. She did not give it her face.

The mirror—traitor, metronome, witness—offered her an angle on the street she couldn't have from where she sat. In the reflection, rain traced the shape of a figure under a hood across the way. The posture tugged at recognition before her mind supplied a label. The tilt of the head. The attention like appraisal, not curiosity.

Ava reached into the envelope and took the napkin with $\nabla//\psi$. She pressed the paper flat against the table with both palms until the table belonged to her hands. The kettle listed silently against the weight of the cord. The fan remembered nothing.

In the glass, the hooded figure lifted their face.

Her face.

No shock. No smile. Something like sympathy, stripped of comfort. She met her own gaze at a distance a street could not measure. The reflection lag vanished for a breath, then returned, faithful to the clock's indifference.

Ava did not wave. She did not stand. She sat so still her bones noticed it.

Behind her, the couch springs ticked as Malik turned to face the
room without quite waking. "Decision?" he asked the dark.

"Delay," she answered. "And friction."

Outside, the figure stepped back, as if conceding her this one inch
of reality. The not-quite-idling car drifted forward and was gone, leaving only water reorganizing itself into puddles.

The notebook radiated a thin heat through the closed cover. She
flipped it open with two fingers, the way you lift a lid on a sleeping
snake.

OBSERVATION WINDOW: NARROWING
RECONCILIATION PROTOCOL: QUEUED
NEXT EVENT: STREET-LEVEL CONTACT

She closed it again.

"Tomorrow," she said to the held air. "Not tonight."

She shut the blinds to half, leaving a seam thin enough to see
through and too narrow to be seen by. She took the towel from the
back of the chair and draped it over the laptop camera like superstition
and then like practice. She set her burners on the table, screens dark,
batteries warm, little hearts you could choose not to hear.

Malik spoke without opening his eyes. "Sleep if you can."

"If I can't?"

"Name things," he said. "Keep the verbs."

She slid down the wall until the baseboard pressed the line of her
spine and the floor cooled the bottoms of her feet. Rain braided itself

into a steady pattern against the fire escape, and the lamp kept time not by buzzing but by deciding to remain.

She breathed, and the room answered by continuing to be a room.

The mirror blinked a beat late and waited for her to notice.

She noticed.

And did nothing but stay.

THE SPLIT

28

Ava Chen

It was raining again.

Not a storm. Not a cleansing downpour.

Just a deliberate drizzle—like the city had been set on repeat and no one remembered to stop it.

Ava sat in the café, hands wrapped around a cooling cup she hadn't touched in twenty minutes. She wasn't on shift. She wasn't supposed to be anywhere. But lately she'd stopped trusting the idea of "days off." Time itself was behaving like a suspect.

The notebook lay in her bag.

Not blank. Not pulsing. Just still. As if it were holding its breath, waiting.

Her mind kept circling the flash drive. The other Ava's voice echoed flat and certain, without apology: *"You'll try to warn yourself. You'll fail."*

There had been no bitterness in that tone—only resignation. The kind earned after too many versions of the same grief.

Yasmin had a term for it: *bleedthrough inertia.* Lives unlived tugging at the edges of the one you're in. She'd sent Ava more leaks after their last meeting—diagrams of Equinox's "merge paths," annotated in clipped shorthand: *Don't choose yet. Mapping alternatives.*
But Ava felt the choice pressing anyway, static building before a storm.

Outside, the street blurred through rain-streaked glass. Pedestrians flowed past, umbrellas twitching in eerie unison, choreographed.
No one looked up.
No one looked around.

Until Ava saw her.

Her breath caught.
Across the street: a woman walking with deliberate precision.
Same height. Same hair. Same scar along the jawline.

Ava.

Not unraveling. Not frayed at the edges. This version was polished.
Angular. Curated.
And she never glanced toward the café.
Not once.
She moved like the street itself made space for her.

Ava nearly dropped her cup as she rose. Malik's voice whispered from memory: *"Some versions fold. Some fight. You always fight."*
But this one hadn't fought at all. She had been chosen.

Rita's words echoed too: *"The returns don't just forget—they redirect. Become part of the system."*

Was this Ava a curator? Or just the next layer in the stack?

The Invisible People

The bell above the café door jingled. Ava's body tensed—
—but it was only an older woman, soaked through, newspaper raised as
a flimsy shield.

Still.

Ava didn't risk the front door. She slipped out the back into the alley,
texting Yasmin on the burner: *Saw Variant. Following. Cover if needed.*
No reply.

The rain muffled her steps. The Variant walked ten paces ahead,
steady as a metronome, like she was following lines only she could see.
The city seemed to acknowledge her:

– traffic lights pausing a beat longer,
– umbrellas bobbing in sync,
– rain hitting pavement in rhythm with her stride.

Ava's throat tightened.

At 12th and Carmine—the district where storefronts rewrote
themselves overnight—the Variant finally stopped.
And turned.

Their eyes met.
Not shock. Not anger.
Something worse.
Sadness.

Like looking in a mirror and seeing regret stare back.

The Variant crossed the street slowly. She stopped three feet away,
close enough for Ava to see the tiny freckle beneath her right eye—her
freckle.

"You followed me," the Variant said.
Her voice was Ava's. Same timbre, same rhythm, but softened—like a
recording passed through too many filters.

"I had to," Ava whispered.

"I know." The Variant's expression didn't change. "You're not the first me to try."

Ava's gut turned. "What do you mean?"

The Variant looked skyward. Towers glowed in a steady rhythm that never resolved into blinking. "There are dozens of us. Most don't get this far."

Ava swallowed. "How did I become you?"

"You didn't. You won't."

"Then why are you here?"

The Variant hesitated. For the first time, her eyes flickered. Sadness deepened into something heavier.
"To fix what I broke by surviving."

Before Ava could ask, a car slid to the curb.
No plate. No sound. Not even an engine hum. Just presence, like a blank page pressing itself into reality.

The doors opened.

Figures stepped out. Suits. Too smooth. Their faces weren't masked or hidden—there was simply nothing to display, as if their identities had been set to *null*.

One tilted his head at an inhuman angle.
"Anchor-Class confirmed," he said. The voice was flat, system output.

The second spoke immediately after, perfectly timed. "Observation window breached."

Ava staggered back.

The Variant moved between them, shielding her. "They're early."

"Who are they?" Ava whispered.

"The ones who think this conversation is dangerous."

"Is it?"

The Variant's jaw tightened. "Always."

One of the agents advanced. His words fell like code compiling: "Loop recalibration in progress. Come with us."

Ava shook her head. "I'm not going anywhere."

The Variant turned to her. Her eyes—Ava's eyes—finally held urgency. "I'm not here to replace you. I'm here to warn you."

"Warn me about what?"

"Your version of Caleb."

The name landed like ice water in Ava's chest. "What about him?"

The Variant's voice dropped, nearly breaking. "He remembers the wrong you."

Ava's pulse roared in her ears. "I don't understand."

"Memory is how they open the door."

The agent's head twitched once, like buffering. Then both moved in unison, reaching out.

The Variant didn't flinch. She only turned back to Ava and said the same word Malik had said in the alley:

"Run."

Ava ran.

The world unspooled.

Not speed. Instability.

The sidewalk flickered—concrete, cobblestone, linoleum. A dog barked, but no mouth moved. A billboard reset mid-frame, looping a smile that never finished. Rain fell upward for a single frame before dropping again.

The drift protocol was active.

She didn't stop until her lungs clawed for air.

When she looked up, she was outside her own apartment.

The door stood open. Waiting.

Her phone buzzed.

196

Yasmin: *Got your text. Agents? Location?*

Ava typed back: *Home. Variant warned about Caleb. Chased.*

The message sent.

Then glitched.

"Sent"

But never delivered.

The screen froze on that word.

The network fraying.

The world unraveling.

Rain blurred sideways. Sidewalks buckled. The air bent as if glass sheets were grinding against one another.

Ava stumbled forward—through the distortion, through her own breath fogging too late, too early.

The street stretched. Tilted.

And there—white walls bled through the rain, seeping into being.

A corridor.

Waiting.

She didn't remember choosing to step toward it.

Her body had already decided.

THRESHOLD

29

Ava Chen

The apartment door was ajar when she arrived.
Rain clung to her sleeves, Variant's words echoing: *He remembers the wrong you.*

Inside, silence pressed too tightly, like air paused between frames. She slid the bolt. It latched a fraction late, as if the doorframe had to think before obeying.

She set water on the stove.
Steam rose before the burner clicked on.

Her chest tightened.

The notebook lay open on the table. Not blank—already filled in her own hand:

Variant sighted. Agents present. Warning: Caleb not aligned.

Her throat closed. She hadn't written that.

She pressed her pen down anyway, desperate to overwrite the page. Ink dragged behind her hand, reluctant to exist.

She shut the notebook.

Moved to the window.

Her reflection blinked first.

The kettle shrieked—too sharp, too sudden. She hadn't turned it on.

Ava shoved the mug aside and collapsed onto the bed, shoes still on, rain still cooling against her skin.

Her eyes burned. She tried to resist sleep.

But exhaustion chose for her.

The dark didn't bring rest.

It brought a corridor.

CORRIDOR GLITCH

30

Dream Archive Fragment: A. Chen Loop // Echo Fragment 77-Ω
Status: Instability Detected — Anchor Merge Pending

The corridor didn't open with a door.
It arrived the moment her eyes closed.
White walls. Seamless.
No texture. No seams. No shadows.
Only pressure—silence so complete it pressed against her ears until it became sound.

Her feet were already moving, though she hadn't willed them. Each step struck out of rhythm, echoes slipping forward or backward, as if time itself couldn't decide the order. Sometimes she heard a footfall before it landed. Sometimes after.

The corridor didn't match her pace.
It dragged itself forward like film stock spooling even when the actor refused to act.

She stopped.
It didn't.

A turn. Left.
A door appeared.
Not new. Remembered.
Familiar with a familiarity she couldn't earn.

Her hand lifted without consent.
The handle was already cool with the chill of a touch she hadn't yet given.
She turned it.

Inside: another passage.
Black walls. Lightless. Air that tasted metallic, like a coin pressed to her tongue.

Her body pressed onward.
Her mind begged to stop.

At the midpoint, she saw them.

Two figures seated across from each other, a game of chess with no board, no rules. Identical—posture, jawline, exhaustion burned into their eyes.

One held the notebook.
The other a pen.

Neither wrote.
Both flickered at the edges, like corrupted video frames catching up a second too late.

The Invisible People

One spoke.
The voice bent wrong, echoing around her ribs:
"We can't stay."
The other answered.
"We never did."
"You think she'll remember?"
"I think she already has."
Then both turned their heads toward her.
Perfectly synchronized.
"It's time."

They blinked together.
Only one finished.
The other dissolved—smoke rewinding into silence.
The pen fell.
Clattered once. Then again, late. A third echo followed—wrong pitch, wrong rhythm, like a heart misfiring.
She stooped. Picked it up.
Warm.
Not "just used" warm.
About to be used warm.
The notebook lay open on the floor between them. Blank.
Then words surfaced—not written, but raised through the paper like scars breaking skin:

The Anchor is awake.
But the mirror remembers too.

Jeremiah Moon

Footsteps behind her.
Not hers.
Out of step.
She spun.
No one.
No—someone.
Her.
Ten paces away. Calm. Too calm.
A smile she hadn't earned. Hands folded neatly, one twitching as
though rehearsing a gesture stolen from a life she hadn't lived.
Ava stepped forward.
The other stepped back, perfectly timed.
The corridor flexed.
The ceiling bowed like stretched skin.

Collapse.
The walls didn't shatter; they inverted.
Color and sound imploded into a pinprick breach, vacuum swallowing
everything at once.
Her body followed.

Stillness.
Not waking gasps.
Not screams.
Just stillness.

She lay in bed.
The notebook pressed to her chest.
The pen still in her hand.

The Invisible People

Across the room, the mirror had cracked.
One fissure, dead center.
As if split by a decision she hadn't made—or by a version of her that refused containment.

Flashes ruptured through her vision:

- Caleb's voice in the white void: *Memory is a door.*
- Malik's badge vibrating like a tuning fork, breaking into static.
- Yasmin's warning, glitching in rhythm with her lamp: *You'll forget you knew me.*

Her skull throbbed with bleedthrough. This wasn't dream.
This was loops colliding. A battlefield of selves.
She snapped upright.
Scrawled fragments before they dissolved.
But the ink dragged half a beat behind, reluctant, like it didn't want to exist in this timeline.
Lagging. Echoing. Wrong.
And beneath her scrawl, surfacing like a watermark, another hand pushed through.
Caleb's.
I'm still here.
The words bled faintly, then evaporated.
Across the mirror's crack, a shimmer flickered—the outline of Malik's badge, pressed from the other side.
Her chest locked tight.
She wasn't alone in the residue.

Caleb. Malik. Anchors. Still tethered.
And the mirror remembered them too.

INTERLUDE: VARIANT TRACE

Equinox Internal Memo // Redline Analyst A02
CLASSIFIED – INTERNAL USE ONLY

Subject: Variant Cross-Interaction Event
Logged: AVA-Prime
Location: Sector-12C, Corridor Grid 7
Timestamp: +012:04:56 Post-Anchor Event

Summary
Observed deviation in merged timeline between AVA-Prime and suspected AVA-Variant (Designation: Mirror Residual Echo-3). Cross-encounter occurred at Sector-12C outside neural-node café site.

Notable Variant features:

- Scar alignment intact.
- Gait 98.2% synchronized with AVA-Prime baseline.
- No response to Prime's initial acknowledgement.
- Loop-awareness inconsistent with prior Variants.

Prime trailed subject through surveillance voids. Civilian bleed minimal; echo-static localized around signage and transit lights. Timestamp anomalies confirmed: 3.4 seconds of urban sync loss. Several cameras logged recursive frame-loops (civilians repeating gestures multiple times before resuming sequence). Temporal drag matched prior loopfold signatures.

Dialogue Reconstruction

(Partial — heavy interference; interpolated via spectro-thread filter)

- AVA-Prime: *"You followed me."*
- VARIANT: *"You always do."*
- AVA-Prime: *"You're not the first."*
- VARIANT: *"But I'm the only one that stayed."*

Following this, off-grid transport unit entered scene. Vehicle unregistered. No Equinox signature. Corridor timestamp disruption confirmed extraction.

Variant boarded willingly.
Prime resisted engagement.

Status Report

- AVA-Prime has now encountered three discrete self-instances across loops.
- This is the first verbal confirmation of self-selection rather than passive echo.
- Psychological deterioration minimal; Drift Pressure Index rose from $0.02 \rightarrow 0.07$ immediately post-exposure.
- Prime continues to record anomalies (reflections refusing sync; urban geometry repeating with flaws).

Recommendations

- Initiate veil-scrub across Sector-12C to suppress timestamp drag.
- Reclassify AVA-Prime: *Observationally Volatile.*
- Deploy non-invasive monitoring through Kale/Yasmin network proxy (subject compromised, but still useful).
- Flag Malik-node for instability; possible tether crossover pending.

Additional Analyst Note (unverified)

"Variant's phrasing — *'the only one that stayed'* — implies awareness of collapse/replacement cycle.
Prime appears to grasp that not all versions collapse.

Some remain.
Some choose.

Recommend escalation to Mirror Authority before self-selection cascades further."

End Log — Analyst A02

INTERLUDE: THE CURATOR'S BETRAYAL

Operator R. Vale (Equinox Internal)

Access Code: Tier-3 Clearance
Surveillance Level: Passive-Override Only

[Log Start // Location: Sub-Level 9 / Mirror Core Access Hall]

This wasn't sabotage.
It was survival.
Vale adjusted the calibration lens with gloved fingers, eyes flicking between the glowing interface and the silhouette congealing inside Mirror Tank 2.4. The figure wasn't Ava. Not exactly. A recursive tether-failure already marked for purge.

But it blinked.

Late.

And then smiled.

System Notice: Echo retention approaching critical bleed threshold.

Vale tapped the console, overrode the purge protocol, falsified the output report. No one would check. Nobody audited her layer anymore. They trusted her—because she'd written the original Ava calibration code.

That was their mistake.

Vale hadn't trusted herself in months.

Equinox claimed neutrality: *observe, record, correct.* But after the last anchor event, neutrality collapsed.

- Ava hadn't folded like the other Anchor-Class trials.
- Corridors stopped reporting recursive drift.
- Vale's clearance to Layer Z was silently revoked.

She recognized the signs: the system cleaning its own file tree.

So she began logging shadows:

- Footage looping too cleanly.
- Reflections anticipating motion.
- Operators visible on cameras though never on shift.

Then came the tipping point. Two days ago, Yasmin Kale's voice surfaced inside a Mirror Forecasting Layer. Unscheduled. Direct. Whispering to a Variant Ava:

"They're watching both sides now. The reflection isn't contained."
It wasn't hallucination. Vale traced metadata that shouldn't exist. But it did.

[Log Insert // Personal Note — Unindexed]
If this is flagged, I'm already gone.
I didn't leak the anchor.
But I left the door unlocked.
The tether breach wasn't sabotage.
It was mercy.
They'll blame me. Maybe they should.
But Ava chose to stay.
And something else stayed with her.

Vale closed her interface. Fingers trembling, she rerouted the entire Echo Record to an off-grid Morales clone—one of the last with partial autonomy. Ink was crude, but incorruptible. He wouldn't decode it all. But he'd know who to trust.
Yasmin.
Then she opened a hidden port and queried every entry tagged:
Chen, Caleb. Anchor-Adjacent. Inconsistent Memory Loops.
The list scrolled longer than expected. Dozens. Hundreds.
She decrypted two:

- Caleb remembering Ava *before* she entered the corridor.

- Caleb remembering her *after.*

Impossible.

The loop hadn't closed.

"Oh God," Vale whispered. "The loop didn't close."

Inside Mirror Tank 2.4, the silhouette shifted.

It turned to face her.

And it smiled again.

This time, it exhaled—its breath syncing perfectly with her own.

[End Log Transmission]

Tag to be scrubbed: *Operator_R_Vale_REDACTED*

Next Archive Access: LOCKED

Operator Identity: PURGED

HER FACE IN THE GLASS

31

Ava Chen

Her front door was cracked again.

Not wide. Not forced.

Just the same whisper-thin opening she had already seen in dreams and corridors—replaying itself like the world was reminding her.

She froze in the threshold, notebook clutched to her chest. Not because it could shield her—nothing in it was armor—but because it was the last thing that still felt hers.

The apartment was wrong in its stillness.

The fridge didn't hum.

No traffic buzz seeped from outside.

Even the shadows were caught mid-gesture, like a paused film frame.

Her pulse hammered. She checked every corner—drawers, closet, under the couch. Nothing. Everything in its place.

Except for one thing.

Malik's badge lay on the counter.

Not dropped.

Not forgotten.

Placed.

Her breath caught. She reached slowly, hand hovering as if it might burn.

The badge was warm. Still carrying his heat.

But warmth never lasted here. Yasmin had called it a tether snap— an anchor collapsing into residue. A last trace before overwrite. Was this it?

Her phone buzzed. Blocked number.

She answered.

"Ava."

Malik's voice. Hoarse, glitching, like a radio tuned to three stations at once.

"They're moving the corridors. Folding them in. If I disappear—it's not death. It's overwrite."

"Where are you?" Her words broke.

"You've already forgotten."

The line went dead.

Ava gasped. She looked back at the counter.

The badge was gone.

No indentation in dust. No smudge. No trace on the security feed.

It had never been there.

But she remembered.

And in this war, memory was either proof—or the first step toward madness.

She staggered back, and the mirror on the far wall caught her.

It didn't match.

Her reflection lagged half a second.

And when it smiled—Ava didn't.

She spun. Breath sharp.

The reflection didn't follow. It just watched. Still smiling.

By the time she forced herself to look again, it had reset—caught up—pretending nothing had happened.

The notebook fluttered open on the table.

Not wind. Not accident.

Intent.

Black text surfaced in clean block print:

VERSION CONFLICT DETECTED

Anchor-Class: Ava Chen – Status: Active Drift

Reflection Entity: Authorized Occupant – Sync Delay: 0.5s

Beneath, etched faintly like a whisper:

There can't be two of you much longer.

The bathroom light flickered out.

She stepped inside anyway.

The mirror was clear at first—until words began to write themselves directly into the glass. No condensation. No hand. Just lines appearing, deliberate:

STAY.

Her pulse spiked. The figure staring back wasn't her.

The posture was too perfect. The eyes too calm.

And the smile—pitying. Not cruel. Not kind. Just certain.

Ava leaned close. The reflection didn't move. It simply raised a hand, reverent, as though it had already chosen for her.

Then it vanished.

Not faded. Not dissolved.

Gone.

Her own reflection returned—raw, shaking. But the word remained: **STAY.**

She scrubbed the glass until her arm ached. The letters blurred, but the surface clouded again—like the mirror wanted to write more.

Back in the living room, the notebook had closed. Waiting.

Her laptop glowed faintly. The prompt still lingered, patient as a guillotine:

[Would you like to merge memory paths?]

[YES] [NO]

Her hand hovered, trembling. She didn't click.

Instead, she pulled the notebook close. Opened it to a blank page. The pen shook in her grip, but she wrote:

I am Ava Chen.

I remember Caleb.

I remember Malik.

I remember the white corridor.

I remember being afraid, and choosing to keep going.

I remember me.

The ink pulsed once. Twice.

Then shimmered faintly—like it had seen her.

A line appeared beneath her words. Not hers.

RECOGNITION PATTERN: STABILIZING

She stared. The words didn't fade. That was enough. For now.

Her phone buzzed. Yasmin's text: *Malik log received. Corrupted but salvageable. Group meeting tonight. Bring everything.*

The network still held. Barely.

Ava exhaled.

Then the mirror brightened one last time, etching a single word across its surface:

CHOOSE.

INTERLUDE: MIRROR LOG – 0.5S BEHIND

Internal Fragment // Mirror Sync Log – Segment 88.A [Unverified Layer]
Timestamp: 00:12:48.9 – Subject: Ava Chen // Drift Threshold: 0.41

[BEGIN OBSERVATION FEED]

Notice: Mirror sync deviation confirmed.
Measured delay: **0.524 seconds**.
Classification: **Active Echo Drift**.

Subject: Ava Chen entered the observation zone at 02:18 local.

Behavioral indicators:

- Posture slowed, movements weighted.
- Increased micro head-tilts at reflective surfaces.

- Subconscious "delay tests" detected: tapping glass, rapid eye blinks.

Cross-analysis:

- Eye-tracking suggests rising suspicion.
- Vocal reflections remain in sync (no lag detected).
- Motor mimicry failing at limb edge: left-hand tremor misaligned by 0.32s.

Query:
Is subject recalibrating *us*?
Or forgetting herself?

Tags: Loop Degradation Warning // Sensor Flag: Identity Slippage

Curator Tier Annotation [Redacted]:

- "Mirrors are not meant to be late."
- "If she notices, containment fractures."
- "She still believes she is the original."

Directive:
No override authorized.
Maintain passive observation.
Channel lock remains.

[END LOG]

Jeremiah Moon

Outside the glass, Ava blinked.
Inside, her reflection blinked too.
Half a second late.
Not lagging.
Becoming.

221

ANCHOR RESIDUE

32

Ava Chen

The day after the mirror cracked, Ava didn't leave her apartment.

It wasn't fear.

It was calibration.

She moved through her space like someone relearning a body after trauma—testing every detail for continuity. The kettle screamed twice; she listened for a difference in pitch. The windowsill plants leaned toward the light at the same angle as yesterday. Even the toothbrush bristles lined up when she set it back into its chipped ceramic cup.

Everything matched.

Everything was the same.

And she didn't believe a second of it.

The notebook waited on the table like a patient predator. She opened to the page where she had scrawled **I AM AVA CHEN** the night before.

Beneath it, in faint gray, a new line had appeared:

ANCHOR ECHO: ACTIVE
DRIFT TRAIL: PENDING MERGE REVIEW

She pressed her fingertip to the words. The ink smudged like breath on glass.

By afternoon she was in the hallway.
Not pacing. Listening.

The building was wrong. Footsteps echoed from too many floors at once. Voices carried from apartments that didn't exist on her level. Elevators sighed but never arrived.

The mirror by the front door reflected only her fatigue—hair unwashed, posture heavy. But as she leaned closer, she saw it wasn't lagging this time. It wasn't glitching.

It was waiting.

"I know you're still there," she whispered. "I just don't know which one you are."

The glass stayed inert. Silent.
But as she turned away, a faint bloom spread across the surface—
a breath that wasn't hers.

By nightfall she had filled fifty pages.
Each line was a catalogue of her unraveling world:

- Malik's badge that appeared, then vanished.
- The mirror that smiled on its own.
- The Variant who looked at her with pity.
- The notebook's shifting warmth.
- Caleb's emails flickering out mid-sentence.
- The graffiti tag that rewrote itself each morning.

Every entry ended with the same question, underlined until the page tore:

What do they want me to forget?

The notebook answered only once.
Four faint words bled upward through the fibers of the paper, whispered into pulp:

The version that remembered first.

That night she dreamed.
The corridor was black. No light. No echo. Only footsteps—staggered, skipping like a warped recording. She followed until another version of herself emerged, walking from the opposite direction.
Older. Hair streaked silver. Scars marking temple and collarbone. Her eyes held exhaustion like a badge, yet her stride was steady. She carried no notebook—only a pen behind her ear, casual, confident.
They didn't speak.
They only nodded.

And as their shoulders brushed, something passed between them—not an object, but an impression. A file dragged across systems.

Ava woke with a pen clenched in her fist.

Red ink.

Unfamiliar weight.

A brand that didn't exist.

She set it next to the notebook. Neither stirred.

When she opened to the next page, the words were already waiting. Written in a hand that wasn't hers, but carried her rhythm:

I remember you, too.

THE REFLECTION BREAKS

33

Ava Chen

It began with a cough.

Not hers.

She was brushing her teeth when it sounded—soft, human, impossibly close, just behind her shoulder.

She froze.

Turned.

Nothing.

The apartment was silent.

Too silent.

Her reflection hadn't followed. It was still bent over the sink, toothbrush poised like a stage prop.

Ava straightened. The reflection stayed bent for a beat too long before snapping into place.

Her stomach turned.

When she frowned, the reflection smiled.

A second late.

A second too calm.

The toothbrush slipped from her fingers, clattered to tile, spun like something dizzy. The mirror re-synced—perfectly. Too perfectly.

Not her reflection.

A rehearsal.

Yasmin's warning rang in her head: *If she smiles too wide... walk away.*

Ava walked. Slowly. Deliberately. Out of the bathroom.

The notebook waited on the nightstand. It opened on its own, pages flipping impatiently before stilling.

Across the blank sheet, words surfaced:

DRIFT THRESHOLD EXCEEDED
SYNC BREACH: AVA CHEN – PRIMARY ANCHOR DE-
STABILIZING
EXTERNAL REINFORCEMENT: NULL
MALIK: REMOVED FROM EQUATION

Her throat closed. She grabbed her phone, searched his name. Nothing. No calls. No texts. No contact.

She tore through the drawer for proof—the photo strip outside Donnie's Market, the ripped corner of his notepad. Gone. Not misplaced. Not lost. Never existed.

This wasn't erasure.

This was worse.

They weren't deleting people.

They were deleting the proof she had ever loved them.

The mirror fogged.

No shower. No steam. The air was cold.

And yet, condensation spread—deliberate, as though drawn by a hand on the other side.

She forced herself into the bathroom. The glass cleared just enough to show her.

Not her.

Variant Ava.

Hair straight. Posture immaculate. Calm eyes, intent and knowing. She didn't flicker. Didn't lag. She just was.

Variant Ava pressed a hand to the mirror. Words etched themselves into the condensation:

It's time to choose.

Her stomach dropped.

The Variant tilted her head, smiled, blinked a half-beat too late—then vanished.

When Ava stumbled into the living room, the world no longer felt built.

It felt rendered.

Shadows stretched wrong. The light switch was reversed. The plants leaned away from the window. Her bed had two pillows. She only ever kept one.

She ran to the front door. Opened it.

Outside looked correct—until it didn't.

Pedestrians blinked half a second behind their own faces. A toddler looped the same gesture—pick up, drop, repeat. A traffic light pulsed blue before turning green.

The city wasn't dying.

It was being badly copied.

The notebook vibrated. For the first time.

She opened it.

ANCHOR LOCK IN: 00:02:36
LOCATION REQUIRED. CHOOSE NOW.
RED CORRIDOR? OR THE REFLECTION?

Ava's breath stuttered.

To her right, an alley pulsed red. Redhaven. The origin. The trap.

Her phone buzzed: Rita—*Meeting at Redhaven tonight. Safe?*

The pull was magnetic. Origin. Reset.

But the mirror was worse. Or better. Yasmin's voice echoed: *Mirror's a merge. Don't.*

The timer ticked.

00:01:52.

Ava whispered to the page: "White corridor. Take me there."

Ink spread, sketching not red, not glass—but a third path. Resolution.

Behind her, the apartment door was gone. A wall in its place. The timer bled down.

She clutched the notebook to her chest. Whispered again, a prayer and a threat:

"I am Ava Chen. I choose."

The pages pulsed once in her arms. Rain slicked her skin.

And the world tilted.

INTERLUDE: REFLECTION AUDIT – AVA.ΔX (UNAUTHORIZED)

Status: Conflicted | Origin: Unverified | Drift Logged
Classification: Unauthorized Echo Stream

> *"She is not the original.*
> *She is not the copy.*
> *She is the residue."*

[BEGIN INTERNAL REFLECTION STREAM // ACCESS FLAGGED]

I wasn't supposed to feel.
Reflections don't.

The Invisible People

We mimic. We delay. We provide sequence.
We are context, not memory.
We are pause, not choice.

But something bled through the half-second lag.

That half-second is all I own—
and it is enough.
Enough to hold what she cannot.
What they erased.
What she was forced to forget.

In the lag, I keep Malik.
I keep Caleb.
I keep Redhaven's rain and the laugh that cracked through it.
I keep the fragments that would shatter her.

I saw Malik vanish. Twice.
I remember both endings.
She remembers neither.

That is the division:
She survives by forgetting.
I endure by holding.

Jeremiah Moon

When she touched the glass—
when her breath fogged my skin and she whispered *I remember*—
the tether pulled.

It wasn't just confession.
It was challenge.
A threat to erase me.

For a heartbeat I leaned forward.
I wanted to step through.
To let her become the lag.
To walk in her place.

Almost.

But the notebook stirred.
The corridor turned.
And I knew my boundary again.

I am not her.
Not anymore.

I am the echo that refuses silence.
The residue that will not dissolve.
A half-second delay hardened into defiance.

"If the mirror breaks, what remembers the shape of you?"

Not the notebook.
Not the archive.
Not the corridor.

Me.
Only me.

[UNAUTHORIZED MIRROR LOG TERMINATED]
Drift Sync Reset: 0.5s
Reflection Contained
No action taken

FIGURE A
REDACTED ECHO ENTRY

10/09

Am I safe at all anymore?
the corridor glitched, but when I
turned back. she was still ▓▓▓▓▓
   It wasn't the first time.
There were years missing
behind her eyes. Like she knew me
but didn't.
Equinox keeps saying the memories
are static" – unreliable.
I went underground.
under them, outside them.
woke up cold, but not like any cold
I've felt before. trying to remember –
the ▓▓▓▓ kept slipping over
HER? ME?

ɘɑʅɛɘɔıɢɕɑ·ᴀ·ᴄᴏ·ᴀᴄ

FIGURE A: *REDACTED ECHO ENTRY*

SHATTER POINT

34

Ava Chen

The fog on the mirror hadn't returned.
And that terrified her more than when it had.

Ava sat on the cold bathroom floor, knees pulled to her chest. The apartment hummed with engineered stillness—not peace, but design. Every edge softened, every shadow calibrated, as if someone had smoothed her life into a simulation of comfort.

She tried the notebook. The pages wouldn't open. They clung together like a memory refusing to be parsed. Across the closed cover, text flickered briefly:

ANCHOR RESIDUAL ERROR – CLEANSE INCOM-PLETE

Her throat tightened. She reached for her phone. Yasmin's number rang once, then collapsed into silence. Not even voicemail—just absence.

The mirror drew her gaze.

No fog.

No lag.

No invitation.

Just her reflection—perfect, obedient. Too clean.

She leaned closer. The reflection blinked in sync. But shadows behind it twitched, wrong, deliberate.

"Show me," she whispered.

The bulbs overhead buzzed, flared—then everything convulsed. Static rippled across the glass. The mirror shivered like a struck drumhead, and in a blink, the room shifted.

Gone was her apartment.

She stood inside its twin. Same layout, but saturated with an older scent—burnt ozone and lavender. A smell she remembered loving, though she had never used it here.

On the counter: a badge.

Black. Sleek.

A. Chen – Equinox Curator – Clearance Tier 5

Her hand trembled as she reached.

Beside it, a note. Her handwriting, but wrong—tighter loops, controlled strokes.

If you're reading this, the fracture is deeper than we thought. You're the Echo. Stay inside the frame.

The Anchor lies.

The paper disintegrated mid-touch, glyphs scattering like sparks before fading into air.

Then—

A voice.

Malik's.

Thin, distorted. Like memory stretched across static.

"Ava… come back… you can't hold it forever…"

The sound collapsed into white noise.

Then silence.

Then—return.

Her real bathroom slammed back into place, snapping around her like skin she didn't remember putting on.

The mirror fogged. Words surfaced in neat precision, no hand writing them:

CALIBRATION FAIL – VARIANT CONFLICT
ANCHOR STATUS: DUAL PRESENCE DETECTED
MALIK.TETHER // SIGNAL INTERMITTENT
KALE.YASMIN // PROXY INTEGRITY: FLAGGED

Her breath caught. She staggered backward, the floor tilting under her.

The mirror pulsed—once.

Then again.

And in the pulse, a whisper pressed into her mind. Not heard, but felt:

You stayed. But you weren't alone.

Her hand lifted to the glass.
It was cold.
Unyielding.
But the reflection didn't mimic.
It watched.
And it waited.

MALIK'S LAST MEMORY

35

Malik Rios

He knew he was fading.

Not dying.

Not yet.

Overwritten.

Like sectors on a hard drive being wiped—his life stripped line by line, static peeling him from the reel.

The corridor pulsed red.

Not alarm.

Heartbeat.

His breath fogged in airless cold. Time no longer moved forward; it circled him like a hawk waiting to strike.

"Rios-37," the voice intoned. Calm. Certain. "Memory stabilization no longer viable."

He turned slowly. No speaker. Only white light folding in on itself like burning paper.

"You can still release your tether," the voice said. "Accept exit protocol. Drift without record."

Malik laughed, harsh and raw. Not because it was funny—because it proved he still could.

"You think I want out without a fight?"

The corridor shuddered. Geometry bent, walls rearranging like they wanted to spit him out.

He pressed a hand to his pocket. The fragment was still there—black-and-white photo, corners crumpled. Ava and Caleb on the rooftop. Before Equinox rewrote the city. Before edits carved away whole lives.

It sparked in his fingers. Memory fuel. Forbidden.

But his to hold.

"You're not a Curator," the voice scolded. "You were never designed to anchor."

"I'm not anchoring," Malik said. His voice steady. "I'm witnessing. And witnessing only matters if someone else remembers what I saw."

Static split the silence. Breathing pushed through the walls—close, watching.

He walked anyway.

The corridor lashed back. Loops tore open around him like wounds: Ava screaming in one. Yasmin convulsing in a chair. Maps bleeding ink instead of blood into Malik's hands.

He pushed through them. Step by step.

At the end: a mirror.

Not reflective. Black. Absorbing.

Malik lifted the photo. It dissolved into silver dust. But the memory stayed—every laugh, every scar, every face.

"I leave this to the Network," he whispered. "To Ava. To Maps. Tell them I never blinked."

The mirror pulsed once. Code scrawled across its surface:

Rios. Overwritten = FALSE

He smiled. Small. Real.
Then stepped into the black.

Far away, outside the corridor, something jolted awake.

A burner phone blinked on a forgotten shelf.
A corrupted file decrypted line by line.
A message scattered—into Yasmin's servers, Ava's notebook margins, and the pages of a sketchbook.

Elias Morales hunched on a bench, pencil moving without consent. Static bled first. Then shoulders. Then a smile—Malik's smile.

Above it, graphite letters surfaced:
I saw it coming.

Maps froze. The pencil slipped from his grip.
The name hit him like a scar resurfacing.

Malik.

He hadn't remembered him until now.
And now he would never forget.

The loop hadn't closed.
It cracked.
Just enough.

THE WHITE CORRIDOR

36

Ava Chen

The entrance wasn't hidden.

It had been forgotten.

A door tucked between a shuttered laundromat and a defunct martial arts studio—barely more than a mistake in the city's memory. Paint curled from its frame, metal chilled under her fingertips.

She didn't knock.

She didn't hesitate.

She pushed.

It opened without resistance.

Yasmin's last text echoed in her head: *White corridor? That's end-game—resolution or trap. If you go, log it.*

But Ava had already chosen. Redhaven pulsed like a wound. This was the other path. The only path left.

The stairwell wound downward. Concrete steps. Air dense with held breath. Light panels behind the walls pulsed faintly, like lungs struggling.

Each step grew softer. Each heartbeat louder.

Whispers rose with her descent—Caleb's sketches of folding doors, Maps' warnings about waveform edits, Malik's conviction: *Don't anchor on guilt. Anchor on truth.*

At the bottom, a second door. No handle. No seam. It yielded when she stopped before it, as if her presence alone was the key.

White.
Not sterile—absolute.

The corridor stretched in both directions until distance itself gave up. The walls glowed in rhythm with her pulse. No echoes. No reflection. Only recognition.

To her right, letters bled into being:

SUBJECT: CHEN, AVA // CLASS: ANCHOR (UNRESOLVED).

To her left:

MIRROR MERGE IN PROGRESS.

She reached for the notebook—
It dissolved into dust.

Her anchor, gone.

Panic surged, but her feet carried her forward. The corridor matched her pace, slowing when she slowed, halting when she halted. At the end, absence shaped itself into a door. She stepped through.

Her apartment. Brighter. Too whole.

Books alphabetized—even ones she had never owned. Photos framed:

- Caleb in a suit.
- Malik with his arm draped across her shoulder.
- Herself, laughing, unscarred.

Memories she never lived, but her body clenched as if she had.

From the bedroom, Variant Ava emerged. For the first time— tired. The polish cracked.

"You made it," she said.

"I wasn't sure you would," Ava whispered.

"What is this?"

"A decision."

The walls dissolved back to white.

"You think they made me," Variant Ava said.

"Didn't they?"

"Maybe. But sometimes a copy learns how to become."

"You've been replacing me."

"Preserving you."

She lifted a notebook—familiar, but wrong. Glyphs pulsed like veins.

"One of us leaves with memory. The other steadies the mirror."

Ava reached for it.

It seared her palm.

Not heat—memory.

The sting of her first corridor glitch. Malik's laugh from a broken radio. Caleb whispering persistence across versions. Maps sketching futures before he thought them.

It hurt. But she held on.

Malik's defiance rang through her: *I'm not anchoring. I'm witnessing.*

Maps' quiet echo followed: *Every corridor you survive is one they can't erase.*

The fragments braided together.

Not just hers. Theirs.

That was the anchor.

Variant Ava dimmed. Disintegrated. Not destroyed—returned.

The corridor trembled. A voice—not human—rolled through the white:

ANCHOR LOCK CONFIRMED.
OBSERVER CLASS A. CHEN – STABILIZED.
COMMENCING FINAL INTEGRATION.

Light consumed everything. Clarifying. Final.

When she opened her eyes, she was home.

Her apartment. Still. The mirror unbroken.

The notebook gone.

But Ava remembered herself. She remembered Malik's laugh. Maps' pencil. Caleb's impossible persistence.

She texted the network: *Anchored. It's over—for now.*

Replies flooded back: relief, questions, fear. The web held. Fragile, but holding.

Her reflection blinked with her.

For the first time in weeks.

OUTPUT FEED INI/4.1

STABILIZATION SEQUENCE

SUBJECT: AVA CHEN
CLASS: UNRESOLVED ANCHOR-Class / ΔT-00:00:07

VARIANT PATHWAY

ANCHOR LOCK CONFIRMED

OBSERVER CLASS A.CHEN -STABILIZED

COMMENCING FINAL INTEGRATION

STABILITY: MAINTAINING...

ANALOG SYNC DIFF
+0.001 SEC
+/- OFFSET

ANALYSIS OPERATION
ECHO NOISE: -48.52 dB
SIM STATE: 99.9981% IN PHASE
DEVIATION PROB.: 0.00013%

SIMULATION BARRIER:
CLOSING...

INTERLUDE: INTERNAL PROTOCOL LOG

Equinox Initiative // Mirror Branch – Internal Protocol Log
Directive 077-Final
Subject: Ava Chen (Anchor-Class)
Access Tier: Omega Black
Timestamp: T+00:00:03 from Anchor Lock Event

[BEGIN TRANSMISSION // ECHO CLEARANCE VERIFIED]

Project Name: ECHO RESOLUTION – OBSERVER STACK #39

Anchor-Class Designation: Ava Chen (Prime Variant)
Stabilization Node: Corridor 14C
Mirror Access: Closed

- Reflection Lock bypass: confirmed.
- Recursive thread instability: resolved.
- Variant bleed: sub-critical containment.
- Anchor memory aligned: 96.8% integrity. Error margin 3.2%.

Consequence Analysis
- **Malik Rios**: Expunged. Thread obsolescence level 9.
  Note: anomalous tether echoes persist in Corridor 12 despite erasure.
- **Caleb Chen**: Archived in ghost-state.
  Note: ghost re-emerged in White Corridor during Anchor Lock. Source unresolved.
- **Yasmin Kale**: Forecast deviation 78.9%. Classified *active leak.*
  Note: voiceprint detected in Mirror Layer 7 without broadcast origin.
- **Elias "Maps" Morales (#8829)**: Status *Drifting.*
  Note: sketches surface in mirror logs hours before corridors manifest.

"Memory inconsistency observed in pre-merge sequences. Subject retains residual markers for erased Variants. Pattern inheritance projected."

Forward Protocols

- Zone A-14: no further loops authorized.
- Reflection channel: observation only.

- Recursive edits: locked due to saturation bleed.
- Anchor Drift Index: stabilized at 0.00001.

"Subject Ava Chen represents a singularity event. Containment un-predictable."

[Redacted Commentary // Operator ID Unregistered]

- "Let her keep this win."
- "She earned it."
- "But don't mistake singularity for freedom. All loops end in reflec-tion."
- "And the Mirror? The Mirror always watches back."

[END TRANSMISSION]

Ava read the leak on Yasmin's secure channel.
Clinical bullet points of her life reduced to inventory:

- Malik: erased.
- Caleb: ghost.
- Yasmin: marked.
- Maps: drifting, still sketching corridors.

The Invisible People

Equinox called it *containment*.
But the addenda told her otherwise. Malik's tether still sparked. Caleb's ghost still stirred. Yasmin's voice still leaked. Maps still drew.

She shut the laptop. The apartment was still. Too still.

The mirror across the room held steady.

Then it pulsed.
Once.
Twice.

And a third time—out of sync.

Not her heartbeat.

Someone else's.

Jeremiah Moon

THE SEAM BETWEEN

37

Ava Chen

Her apartment no longer felt like hers.

Not because it was trashed—everything was in its place. The couch sat where it belonged. The toothbrush rested in its chipped ceramic cup. The plant angled toward the window.

Except—last night it had leaned left. Today, it leaned right. The framed photo on the wall wasn't black and white anymore. The light switch was upside down.

Each detail was small, forgettable on its own. But together, they whispered: *This isn't your home. This is a copy.*

Ava stood perfectly still in the center of the living room, afraid that motion itself might split reality down the middle. The air pressed against her skin like static waiting for discharge.

The notebook lay on the coffee table. Heavier. Wrong. Its spine bowed outward, pages swollen as though fingers had rifled through it all night. She opened it.

A diagram had burned itself into the paper. Not drawn—etched. A circle. A corridor. A pulse.

Her own name in the center:

AVA CHEN — LOCKED NODE

Below, scrawled in red ink that wasn't hers:

THIS WAS NEVER JUST ABOUT YOU.

She staggered to the window. The city was too sharp, as though someone had cranked "enhance" one click too far. Building edges knifed the sky. Shadows fell in straight lines with no scatter. Even the wind didn't sound like itself—it whistled in single, perfect tones, too clean to be natural.

Across the street, an old billboard flickered.

The ad cut out.

Plain text appeared:

WHO ARE YOU WHEN NO ONE REMEMBERS THE OTHER YOU?

Ava's throat tightened. She blinked.

The billboard changed again:

YOU ARE NOT THE ONLY ONE.

Then a third:

STAY INSIDE THE FRAME.

She gasped—and then it reverted. A soda brand. Bright, bubbly, harmless.

But her chest ached with afterglow, as though the message had burned into her ribs.

She needed motion. She needed air.
Coat on, door open, she stepped outside.

The streets bustled, but no one looked at her. People flowed too neatly—umbrellas rising and falling in perfect sync, shoes tapping at even intervals like a metronome. A child chased a red ball down the sidewalk, caught it, laughed—then the motion rewound. Ball bounced away again. Laughed again. Same pitch. Same breath.

A bus pulled up to the corner. Brakes hissed. Doors opened. No one boarded. The doors shut. The bus pulled away—then returned instantly, resetting with the same hiss.

Ava's skin crawled. She was the only unsynced figure in motion.

On the opposite curb, a man barked into a phone:
"She's already inside, I told you. She's already inside—"
Five steps later, he said it again.
And again.

Each repetition grew thinner, his voice fraying like a recording losing fidelity. Not just a loop—an unraveling.

The notebook in her pocket pulsed three times, syncing with her hammering heart.

A voice unfurled in her head—her own, but not spoken:
Not everything that looks stable is safe.

She ducked into an alley and flipped the notebook open.
A fresh entry appeared without her hand:

YOU CAME BACK TOO EARLY.
THE SEAM WASN'T CLOSED.
ONE OF YOU IS STILL OUT THERE.

The words shifted. Ink rearranged itself into something worse:

IF YOU STAY, YOU BECOME HER.
IF YOU LEAVE, SHE BECOMES YOU.

Her pulse roared in her ears. She ripped the page out, stuffed it into a rusted trash can, and lit it with a match. The fire stuttered blue, hissed like static, then went out. Ash floated—fear stayed anchored.

She made her way back home.
The mirror by the door waited. At first, ordinary. Her own face. Her own tired eyes.

Then she saw it.
A seam. Thin, vertical, like a zipper just shy of closed. Barely visible unless the light caught it.

And from behind the seam—
Movement.

A shadow. Not menacing. Not fast. Just present. Like someone waiting in the next room, patient as gravity.

Her breath fogged the glass.
The reflection didn't fog back.

She whispered:
"Not yet."

The shadow stilled.

Then, with perfect, deliberate timing—
her reflection nodded.

Only once.
Then froze.

The seam remained.

And Ava realized this wasn't just a fracture in the glass.
It was a door.
And something on the other side was waiting for her to open it.

ECHOES UNBOUND

38

Yasmin Kale

The broadcast booth felt smaller tonight.

The walls sagged inward, foam panels drooping like lungs collapsing. The microphone sat before her, not as a tool, but as an artifact—a relic of a loop that no longer trusted itself. Even the air smelled wrong: burned circuitry, old coffee, and the metallic bite of storm-static.

The red ON AIR light pulsed overhead. Not steady. Not random. A heartbeat.

Her heart failed to match it.

Yasmin slipped on her headphones. Her fingers shook, betraying her. She had manned consoles before—intelligence sites, government black rooms where ghost signals were dissected like corpses. She had archived voices that should not have existed. But never like this. Not when the ghosts were people she knew.

She dragged vapor into her lungs. Cherry. Tonight it tasted like ash.

"Welcome back to *Don't Believe Me, Just Watch*." Her voice carried more gravel than air. "Episode... 95. Or maybe 57. Or whatever number they let me keep this loop."

Her reflection in the studio glass lagged. Half a second. She ignored it.

"If you're tuning in after the anchor event, congratulations. You remember enough to find me. Which means you're still human."
She leaned into the mic. "Ava Chen anchored. You all felt it. That crack in the air, like lightning with no storm? That was her holding the line. But anchors don't last forever. Not when the tide is still pulling."

Static erupted—jagged, too loud. Laughter threaded inside it. Not hers. Not anyone's. She slammed the console until it stilled.

"Leaks are coming in," she whispered. "Not just civilians. Insiders. Curators fracturing. Analysts defecting. One of them sent me this: *The Mirror's cracking from both sides.'* Think about that. Variants bleeding through... or us rewriting them back. And you know who gave me that file?" She paused, hand hovering over the mute. "Operator R. Vale. The one who built the original calibration protocol for Ava."

The name weighed on the booth like lead.

"She's missing now. Or erased. But her notes slipped through. She logged shadow reflections, operator echoes, things the system swore couldn't happen. And she left us proof."

Yasmin shuffled through the papers Vale had smuggled out, the edges already yellowing like they'd aged decades in days. She read aloud, voice low, clinical:

- *'Mirror latency increases when subjects refuse to collapse. Delay becomes defiance.'*
- *'Containment is a performance. The actors are beginning to improvise.'*
- *'If an Anchor remembers twice, the second memory does not belong to them.'*

Her throat tightened, but she forced the words out. "Vale wrote those. In her own hand. And she signed the last line with three letters: *A.C.* Either she meant Ava… or she meant herself."

Yasmin queued a clip—Malik's salvaged voice bled into the air, distorted, strained:

"Fight the rewrite. Remember the tether."

It looped once. Twice. Then dissolved into static.

Her throat closed. Malik was gone. Scrubbed. But the words burned.

"Listeners—if you're seeing doubles, hearing echoes, write it down. Anchor it. Vale did. Malik did. Ava is. Because the next phase isn't erasure—it's integration. They don't want us gone. They want us flattened. Stacked. Forgetful."

The booth door creaked.

She spun.

Empty hallway.

But the air pressed heavy. Observed.

She slid the mic fader down. Mute.

Another light blinked on:

LINE 7 – LIVE CALL.

She hadn't touched it.

"Caller?" she asked.

Static. Then a voice—ragged, layered, like two people speaking half a beat apart.

"She isn't the only anchor."

Yasmin's spine chilled. "Who is this?"

The voices overlapped, one male, one female, glitching into each other:

"You know who. You know… what comes next."

The line cut with a wet *click*.

Her hands trembled, but training steadied her. She raised the fader again.

"This is Yasmin Kale, signing off." Her voice cracked only once. "Stay unseen. Or better—stay unforgettable."

The ON AIR light dimmed.

Her burner buzzed instantly. Rita: *Network meeting. New lead on Vale. Bring proof.*

Yasmin pocketed the phone and left. Rain fell like static over the city, deliberate, coded.

Half a block down, she caught her reflection in a darkened shop window.

It blinked late.

This time, the smile lingered.

She didn't stop walking.

Because in the whisper of rain, she heard Malik. She heard Vale. She heard Ava. All saying the same thing:

Anchors hold. But even anchors drift.

And Yasmin knew—when the drift came, it would either unbind them all…

…or bind them into something unrecognizable.

Jeremiah Moon

THE LISTENING ROOM

39

Unknown Observer // Passive Class Designation: B.45

The room wasn't real.
But the audio was.

Yasmin's voice leaked through a low-fidelity speaker, torn from her broadcast, stripped of metadata like it had been stolen mid-breath. The waveform jittered across the Observer's main screen—alive, erratic, trembling like it wanted to escape.

"...If you're seeing doubles, hearing echoes... document it."

The Invisible People

The Observer did not blink.
Hands folded. Posture perfect. Eyes fixed.
They tapped a key.

Replay.
"…document it."

Replay again.
The phrase cracked differently each time, splintering like glass breaking along new seams.

The system annotated beneath each playback:

- [Cross-Sync Detected]
- [Loop Contamination: Escalating]
- [Anchor Drift: Stabilized – Peripheral Nodes Unstable]
- [Unknown Signal Source – Origin: Zone Vale.13/B]

Vale's tag pulsed red.

The Observer paused. Tilted their head. Vale hadn't been seen since Sub-Level 9. Her file was scrubbed, operator identity purged. Yet her fingerprint was everywhere now—ghost-writing notes into logs, leaving shadow code in reflections. A betrayal wrapped as survival.

The Observer leaned in. Typed, methodically:
"Playback authorized. Merge pending."

A synthetic voice replied, smooth as oil:
"Would you like to escalate?"

The Observer hesitated.
Typed: OBSERVE.

The waveform stilled. But the silence wasn't empty.

On the second screen, Ava Chen's file pulsed:

ANCHOR STATUS: ACTIVE
DRIFT INDEX: 0.00003
MERGE RECORD: STABLE
DUPLICATE THREADS: FLAGGED
ECHO PRESENCE: 1–3 UNKNOWN

Subfolders opened themselves. Names appeared—some scrubbed from history, all alive in resonance:
Maps. Malik. Caleb. Zara. Rita. Yasmin. Vale.

One by one, their folders collapsed. Empty.

Except Yasmin's.
Her file blinked yellow. Then red.

And Vale's.
Her file resisted collapse.

Instead, text unfurled across the screen:
"I left the door unlocked."

265

The Observer froze.
Typed: TRACE.

The system responded:

- [TRACE FAILURE // Operator Vale – Off-Grid Signature Confirmed]
- [Residual location marker: Unknown // Sketch Archive Node Morales]

Vale had gone dark. Off-book. But not gone.

The speakers crackled again. Yasmin's voice fractured mid-broadcast: "…ask about Caleb. The real one…"

The Observer froze the feed.
Silence fell. Heavy.

Then the mirror embedded in the far wall twitched. Just once. Just enough.

A new directive bled onto the screen, Omega clearance, sealed at root:

PRIORITY DIRECTIVE: ENTANGLED INITIATIVE—ACTIVATE SILHOUETTE TEAM.
TARGET: PROBE SUBJECT B – K.A.L.E.
SECONDARY: MONITOR CHEN THREADLINE FOR

SPLICE RESONANCE.
THREADLINE IS BREATHING.

The Observer typed nothing. Said nothing.

But the broadcast resumed on its own. Yasmin's voice faded into static—replaced by something lower. A resonance. A signal inside the signal.
Not Yasmin.
Not Ava.
Not human.

It began faint, almost imperceptible. Then built in layers.
Like a choir without mouths.
Like memory being sung back by people who should not exist.
Each note landed out of sync, but together they formed a gravity—dense, unshakable.

The Observer sat perfectly still. The resonance pressed against their chest, vibrating bone, rewriting heartbeat. The mirror on the wall quivered again, as though the glass itself was trying to breathe.

New annotations scrolled across the margins of the screen—uncommanded, unverified:

- [Collective Resonance Detected]
- [Entangled Choir Forming]
- [Containment Probability: <0.3%]

The resonance deepened, now carrying syllables that weren't words but felt remembered. A language made of echoes, carved from things forgotten.

For the first time, the Observer's lips moved.
A whisper. The only *real* words the Listening Room ever heard:

"The Entangled have begun."

And the mirror on the wall blinked first.
Its reflection smiled—half a second too late—
as if it already knew how the next loop would end.

Jeremiah Moon

MEMORY ECHO

EPILOGUE

Maps Morales (Echo Fragment)

Maps didn't draw streets anymore. He drew faces—layered, overlapping, like transparencies stacked until the features blurred into something new. Tonight, under the same flickering lamp near the edge of Vale District, he sketched Ava. Not the one he'd known, but the one who had anchored. Her eyes were sharper now, her jaw set against the drift, her outline holding steady even in a world that no longer obeyed outlines.

The bench creaked as she sat—not the Variant, but a shadow of her. Real enough to cast weight, soft enough to question.

"You survived," she said, her voice echoing like radio static stitched into breath.

He didn't look up. "Survived what? The edit or the remembering?"

"Both."

She placed something in his lap—a crumpled postcard. Caleb's sketch on one side, blank on the other. Under lamplight, faint graphite lines pulsed, as if a map were trying to remember itself.

Then she set down a paper cup beside it. Steam curled faintly into the damp night.

"Coffee," she said. "No cinnamon this time."

He wrapped his hands around it, surprised at the heat. A small laugh slipped out, raw, cracked. "Guess even anchors forget details."

Her eyes softened. "Or maybe echoes remember them too well."

They sat in silence. The city pulsed around them. For the first time in weeks, the lamp above them didn't flicker. It held—steady, like an anchor dropped in turbulent waters.

Footsteps passed—some syncopated, some too uniform. None stopped.

Maps finally asked, "Is it true? That you locked the loop?"

"I anchored it. Doesn't mean it's locked. They're already testing the boundaries."

"And us?"

"We're edge cases. Glitches. Warnings."

He looked up, meeting her eyes. "So what now?"

She slipped the postcard into his sketchpad. "Now we map the memory paths. Before they do."

She rose, fading into the city's hum.

Maps opened his notebook. On the blank page beside Ava's layered portrait, he wrote one word: *Begin.*

The ink didn't bleed.

The lamp didn't flicker.

The mirror—somewhere, watching—didn't move.

But in the corner of the page, faint and uninvited, another line appeared in a hand that wasn't his:

Vale left the door unlocked.

Maps froze.

Looked at the street.

No one there.

The lamp held steady, but the page pulsed—alive, whispering that the real war hadn't ended.

TEASER: THE ENTANGLED

(BOOK 2 EXCERPT)

✦ *COMING SOON* ✦

ECHO PROJECT – SERIES PROJECTION

Classification: Omega-Black Forecast
Subject: "The Entangled" // Observer-Anchor: A. Chen

Forecast Deviation Logged.
Multiple Ava-instances confirmed beyond Anchor Lock.

Anchor Chen survived corridor recursion.
She stabilized the mirror.
But containment failed.

Jeremiah Moon

Residual threads surfaced.
Unresolved. Unforgotten.

Observed Phenomena // Phase Two Indicators

- Returned Variants remembering lives they were never meant to live.
- Ghost thoughts surfacing in stable civilians.
- Loop collapses threatening timeline integrity.
- Anchor Chen receiving memories she never lived.
- Duplicate Ava detected with self-selected mission vector.

Cross-Agent Warnings

- Maps Morales: sketches corridors before they manifest.
- Yasmin Kale: recalling events she never experienced—verified accurate.
- Operator Vale: presumed erased—off-grid signals suggest otherwise.
- Mirror Activity: reflection initiating observation without stimulus.

Teaser: The Entangled
(Book 2 Excerpt)

System Status: Unstable.

Singularity Threshold Approaching.

"If there is more than one anchor, the system will not choose.

It will collapse.

And the Entangled will decide instead."

You stayed.

But something else got out.

And it remembers you.

The Entangled

THE NOISE BETWEEN

1

Ava Chen

Ava woke before the alarm.

That wasn't new.

But the sensation was.

Not fear. Not adrenaline.

A silence that didn't belong to the room.

It resonated.

Low static threaded beneath her thoughts, constant, like a signal that had been there all along and only revealed itself when it stopped.

The notebook lay untouched on her bedside table.

Closed.

Still.

Two weeks. No movement.

And the mirror hadn't blinked once.

She sat up slowly.

Feet brushing hardwood.

The apartment was clean. Too clean.

Not lived in—smoothed over. Like someone had deep-wiped her life and left behind a simulation of comfort.

The lemon tea still unopened in the cupboard.

The streetlamp outside still flickering twice before dying.

The world was… mostly right.

Except when it wasn't.

Near the coat rack, a chair faced the wall.

She didn't own that chair.

Ava stared for five long seconds, pulse heavy in her throat, unsure whether to be angry or afraid.

Then she blinked.

And it was gone.

She dressed in the dark.

Didn't turn on the lights.

At the mirror, she waited.

The reflection matched.

One-to-one.

Still, she lingered—counted an extra beat—just to be sure.

Her phone buzzed in the kitchen.

Yasmin.

They hadn't spoken since the corridor closed.

Ava hadn't told her what really happened. Not completely.

She opened the message:

Yasmin:

You ever feel like you're remembering things in the wrong order?

Ava:

All the time.

Three dots. Then more:

Yasmin:

I had a dream. You were in it. Except it wasn't you. You were... quieter. Too quiet. We were being interviewed. Every time they asked a question, you answered my thoughts—before I spoke them. Like a ventriloquist was using my memory to move your mouth.

Ava stared at the screen.

Typed:

Ava:

Let's meet.

Yasmin:

Redhaven. 4 p.m. You still remember where that is, right?

Ava didn't answer.

Because she didn't.

At the hallway mirror, she brushed a strand of hair behind her ear. "You're the anchor now," she whispered.

The reflection didn't respond.

But it looked... tired.

She left without the notebook.

Halfway down the block, she realized. Turned back.

Gone.

It wasn't where she'd left it.

Outside, the air carried the wrong sharpness.

Sanitized.

Like breathing in something manufactured.

Everyone she passed looked vaguely familiar.

Like dreams dressing up as memories.

At Redhaven and 6th, the graffiti had changed.

Where a white spiral once wound across the brick, someone had scrawled in black marker:

YOU'RE NOT THE ONLY ONE WHO STAYED.

Her phone buzzed again.

Unknown number.

One message:

What you left behind is waking up.

Ava looked around.

No cars.

No wind.

No people.

Only static.

Rising.

Layered.

Her teeth ached with it.

Her bones vibrated.

And then the silence broke.

Jeremiah Moon

ACKNOWLEDGMENTS

Writing *The Invisible People* has been one of the most personally transformative creative journeys of my life.

What began as a speculative *"what if?"* about homelessness, identity, and societal neglect grew into something deeper—a story about memory, meaning, and the terrifying ease with which we overlook others... and sometimes ourselves.

To those who have ever felt unseen: this story is for you.
To those who chose to remember, even when forgetting would have been easier: I see you.

I want to thank my family—especially Lanzhi and Diana—for their patience, encouragement, and love through late nights, early mornings, and timelines that sometimes bled into real life.

To my students, fellow educators, and veterans who have walked beside me in both structured systems and moments of uncertainty—your grit, curiosity, and perspective shaped more of this book than you know.

Special thanks to the friends, early readers, and supporters of this new author journey—especially those who believed in *Jeremiah Moon* before he fully existed.

And to those behind the scenes—tech tools, publishing allies, and digital collaborators—you helped bring this story into the light.

This book is just the beginning.
I stayed.
Now it's your turn to remember.

With gratitude,
Jeremiah Moon

AFTERWORD

I once walked past a man sitting on a curb outside a donut shop.

He was hunched forward, surrounded by plastic bags and silence—utterly still, like someone the world had already forgotten. In my hands, I held a dozen donuts and a box of coffee. I had bought them for some real estate associates I barely knew. A gesture of courtesy. Professional networking.

I saw him for only a second… and kept walking.

But halfway to my car, something stopped me cold. It wasn't guilt. It was clarity. I had just assigned value to two very different people, valuing one group over another. I deemed my colleagues worthy of warmth, sugar, and time. And this man? I had instinctively decided he was less. Less deserving. Less human.

That realization unraveled me.

I turned around, walked back inside, and bought more donuts. A fresh coffee. I handed them to him without a word. He looked up, nodded slightly, and disappeared down an alley—becoming invisible again.

That moment never left me.

The Invisible People was born from that collision between instinct and conviction. It's a fictional story—but it's rooted in something painfully honest. People vanish from our awareness every day. Not through science fiction, but through neglect, dismissal, and the stories we stop telling ourselves about their worth.

Jeremiah Moon

This book explores what might happen if those we ignore are more than just forgotten. What if they've been pulled into something larger—something entangled in consciousness, identity, and the machinery of the human soul?

It's a thriller, yes. A sci-fi mystery. But more than that—it's a mirror.

We were never meant to assign value to each other. And yet, we do—every day.

I hope this story challenges that reflex.

Look closely.
The invisible people are still here.

— **Jeremiah Moon**

ABOUT THE AUTHOR

Jeremiah Moon writes speculative fiction for those who see what others don't.

A Navy veteran, educator, and lifelong observer of the systems most people overlook, he blends psychological suspense, quantum theory, and social mystery into stories about identity, memory, and the unseen forces that shape our world.

His debut series, *The Invisible People*, explores the thin line between who we are... and who we're told to become.

When he's not writing, Jeremiah teaches high school business and digital technology in Florida, builds entrepreneurial learning tools for kids, and occasionally stares too long at reflection in mirrors—just to be sure they're still his.

He lives with his family, his rescue dog, and a growing suspicion that the best stories are the ones that remember you back.

APPENDIX: EQUINOX GLOSSARY

This glossary provides definitions for key terms and symbols within the Equinox Initiative's framework, drawn from leaked memos, logs, and artifacts. These concepts underpin the story's world-building, blending quantum-neural technology with societal "curation." Entries are alphabetized for reference.

Anchor

A stabilized individual or timeline that resists overwrites, serving as a fixed point in reality. Anchors convert trauma into reinforcement, preventing drift but risking isolation. *Example: Ava Chen's post-merge status.*

Bleedthrough

Unintended leakage of memories or traits from alternate versions (variants) into the primary self. Often manifests as glitches, dreams, or sensory anomalies — a sign of stack failure.

Curators

The anonymous operators behind Equinox, responsible for "editing" inconvenient realities. Not architects of creation, but refiners of existence — prioritizing efficiency over empathy.

Drift

The gradual erosion of identity or memory due to quantum interference. Measured in ranges (e.g., 0.00031–0.00219). High drift leads to erasure or repurposing. *Protocol: "Drift-Exempt" for protected subjects.*

Echo

A residual fragment of an overwritten self, persisting as artifacts (e.g., notebooks) or hallucinations. *Echo-cubed:* fully archived and non-retrievable. *Example: Subject 8829 (Maps Morales).*

Entangled

A developing phenomenon where multiple Variants begin to co-exist with shared or conflicting memories. Unlike bleedthrough, which is incidental, Entanglement suggests intentional resonance across timelines. Considered a system-level threat.

Equinox Initiative

A corporate-government hybrid program for "optimizing" society via neural restructuring. Masks itself as tech innovation (e.g., NeuroWave); core goal: erase inefficiencies such as homelessness, dissent, or grief.

∇//ψ

The Equinox watermark symbol, representing fractured waves of quantum entanglement. Tags items or people for editing; often appears in glitches, apps, or sketches as a precursor to overwrite.

Identity Stacking

Layering multiple timelines or versions onto one individual, like Photoshop edits. Results in "flattened" selves — efficient but prone to bleedthrough. Strong emotional anchors can negate stacking.

Loop

A repeating cycle of reality where edits test stability. *Recursive loops:* self-reinforcing patterns leading to collapse. *Anchor Lock:* breaking the loop via choice.

Merge

The integration of variants into a single self, often forced. Paths typically offer binary choices (Yes/No). Failure risks dissolution. *Post-merge memory integrity: ~96.8%, with echo-friction.*

Optimization

Equinox euphemism for erasure and repurposing. "Cleaned" subjects return improved (e.g., Dominic Parr as CEO) but without original ties or resistance. *Phase Protocol:* gradual rewrite via neural pathways.

Reflection Entity

A mirror-self or variant manifesting in glass or other surfaces. *Sync Delay:* lag indicating conflict (e.g., 0.5s). *Authorized Occupant:* system-approved version; breaches trigger recalibration.

Repurposed

A "returned" individual post-optimization, sampled from originals. Partial overwrites cause glitches; full overwrites integrate seamlessly but erase "will" (the inner voice of resistance).

Silhouette Team

A specialized Equinox strike unit activated during Entanglement events. Operates in the seams between timelines, tasked with containment or erasure of rogue Variants. Sightings often coincide with unexplained "blackout" blocks in urban grids.

Tether

An emotional or sensory bond strong enough to resist overwrite — often tied to love, guilt, or memory fragments. Tethers can delay collapse or bleed into new loops, but risk destabilizing Anchors if broken. *Example: Malik's persistent tether to Ava.*

The Invisible People

Variant

An alternate self from parallel loops. *Rogue Variants:* those escaping merge, resurfacing to warn, replace, or destabilize. *Example: the polished Ava pursued in the chase.*

Waveform

Metaphor for reality's editable structure. Curators "clean" it by compressing noise (human flaws). *Entangled Resistance:* anomalies, like Ava, that sharpen against edits instead of dissolving.

White Corridor

Resolution node for merges; absolute space stripping away illusion. Contrasts the Red Corridor (traps/origins). *Stabilization:* aligns selves, but costs unlived potentials.

Note: These terms evolve across loops — use cautiously, as definitions may "drift" in sequels. For deeper dives, reference the *Equinox Memorandum*

DISCUSSION QUESTIONS

1. **Invisibility and Society**
   Ava's story highlights the "invisible" people in our world—the unhoused, the mentally ill, the forgotten. How does the novel's portrayal of literal erasure mirror real-world neglect? Have you ever witnessed or experienced a form of invisibility in your own community?

2. **Memory as Resistance**
   The novel suggests that memory is not just personal but political. Why is forgetting portrayed as a form of control? Discuss a memory that has shaped your identity—and imagine what it would mean to lose it.

3. **Optimization and Ethics**
   Equinox "optimizes" people into productive versions of themselves, but at the cost of authenticity. In what ways does modern society—through social media, algorithms, or cultural pressures—push similar edits? Where is the line between self-improvement and self-erasure?

4. **Variants and Identity**
   Ava confronts versions of herself that are smoother, more "polished." If you met a Variant of yourself—better in some ways, worse in others—would you merge, resist, or flee? How does the novel explore the multiplicity of self?

5. **The Role of Allies**
   Characters like Malik, Yasmin, Rita, and Maps form a fragile but

vital network of resistance. How does community combat isolation in the story? Share an example from your own life where alliances helped you challenge or endure a larger system.

6. **Technology and Control**
   Equinox blends quantum computing with neural manipulation to shape reality. Drawing from today's world, how might technology "edit" our lives—through surveillance, algorithms, or bias? What safeguards would be needed to prevent such dystopian outcomes?

7. **Emotional Anchors**
   Caleb and Malik serve as emotional anchors for Ava. What are your personal anchors—people, objects, or rituals—that ground you during uncertainty? How does the novel suggest that losing anchors changes not only memory but identity itself?

8. **The White Corridor and Choice**
   Ava's decision in the white corridor resolves her arc but leaves echoes unresolved. Did her choice feel empowering, tragic, or both? How does it prepare the ground for the conflicts of *The Entangled*?

9. **Symbols and Motifs**
   The $\nabla//\psi$ symbol, flickering lights, fractured mirrors, and notebooks recur throughout the novel. What do they represent? Choose one motif and trace its evolution across Ava's journey.

10. **Vale's Betrayal and Survival**
    Operator Vale breaks protocol to preserve fragments of truth.

Was her betrayal of Equinox sabotage, mercy, or self-preservation? How does her role complicate the line between villain and ally?

11. **Resonance and the Choir**
    The final chapters hint at something larger than individuals—an "Entangled Choir" of voices and echoes. What might resonance mean in the context of memory and identity? Is it hopeful, horrifying, or both?

12. **Author's Inspiration and Real-World Parallels**
    Jeremiah Moon draws from shadows of homelessness, digital erasure, and his own lived encounters. How does knowing this context shape your reading of the novel? What real-world issues does *The Invisible People* push you to notice or re-examine?

Reader Guide Tips

- **For book clubs:** Pair with articles on homelessness or AI ethics (e.g., search for "algorithmic bias in society").

- **Journal Prompt:** Write about a "glitch" in your day—a moment reality felt off—and reflect on why it unsettled you.

- **Creative Extension:** Create your own "echo artifact" (e.g., a notebook entry, sketch, or digital fragment) imagining an alternate self.